Swimming in Grief

Kit Barrie

Swimming in Grief

First edition

Copyright © 2025 by Kit Barrie

All rights reserved.

Cover Art by Sheilkuroi

Cover Design by Amanda Meuwissen

ISBN Ebook: 978-1-962826-05-1
ISBN Paperback: 978-1-962826-06-8

Contents

Content Warning

This story deals with the immediate aftermath of the traumatic accidental death of a spouse as experienced by the main human character, Reuben. This includes scenes at a morgue and a funeral. Throughout the narrative, Reuben deals with painful grief, panic attacks, suicidal ideations, and other strong emotions. He also talks about the loss of his mother years before to breast cancer and his elderly father currently in a nursing home with degenerative memory issues. His father also passes on page, and there is mention of a funeral.

The main monster character, Glauruss, is a hermaphrodite, and he becomes pregnant and gives birth off-page. He then experiences off-page the sudden death of his child through a violent attack, including scenes of memory flashback. Throughout the narrative, Glauruss deals with depression, suicidal ideations, alcohol addiction, and self-destructive behavior. He voluntarily hospitalizes himself to recover from alcohol addiction.

A side character talks about former drug addiction and emotional abuse of his wife and children.

This story contains explicit, consensual sexual situations between adults and is not meant for children. It does have a happy ending.

Prologue

FabTeacher: Hi there, my name is Kyle. Would you be interested in chatting?

SeaKing Swimmer: sure!

FabTeacher: What's your name?

SeaKing Swimmer: Glauruss

FabTeacher: Does that rhyme with glow or with now?

SeaKing Swimmer: never had anyone put it that way b4.

SeaKing Swimmer: But it rhymes with now.

FabTeacher: I teach middle school English, so pronunciation is always important to me. That's quite the name!

SeaKing Swimmer: thanks!! I guess that explains your user name.

FabTeacher: Yes, indeed! You own Monster Marine Excursions?

SeaKing Swimmer: I do!

FabTeacher: What sort of things do you do?

SeaKing Swimmer: I take people out on the ocean on a boat. If they want to swim I help them swim and keep them safe and I also swim around looking for fish in the area.

FabTeacher: That sounds exciting!

SeaKing Swimmer: It can be. Defintely a different world down there than on land.

FabTeacher: Can you go on land, or out of the water, at least?

SeaKing Swimmer: yes I can! I can walk on land or be out of the water for about a day before I need to get back in the water. I like to walk on the beach.

FabTeacher: So, I have a rather unusual request.

SeaKing Swimmer: ok ??

FabTeacher: My husband, Reuben, is turning 51 in April. He's never been fishing before, so for his birthday, I thought I would rent a boat and take him deep-sea fishing.

SeaKing Swimmer: sounds liek fun

FabTeacher: I hope so! But, what I wanted to ask you specifically, and it's perfectly fine if it's not your thing. We thought it might be fun to try a threesome, and Reuben suggested maybe with a monster.

SeaKing Swimmer: Are you asking me if I'd do a threesome with u and your husband?

FabTeacher: Yes. I hope that's not too forward of me.

SeaKing Swimmer: No, i'm flattered!! Just looking for a one time thing?

FabTeacher: We're only planning on once for now, but if we all have a good time, who knows? We definitely don't want you to feel like we're abandoning you afterward.

SeaKing Swimmer: oh I totly get that! I'm up for us just having a good time.

FabTeacher: That sounds perfect! I will talk to Reuben, and we will get back to you. He's a little shy, but he's excited about trying this!

SeaKing Swimmer: that sounds great! Lmk when you're ready to book so I can leave my schedule open for you.

FabTeacher: Will do!

SeaKing Swimmer: hey kyle, haven't heard from u for a while, and I know Reuben's birthday is coming up soon.. Just wanted to see if you have any detales yet.

SeaKing Swimmer: hi, hope everything is ok. If you changed your mind that's ok but just want to know if you have a plan.

SeaKing Swimmer: Something must have come up but if u want to still get together at sum point lmk!

Chapter 1

Reuben

THE KNOCK ON THE front door startled me. I wasn't expecting anyone, and I knew Kyle had his keys. Plus, he always used the side door; our front door was a little sticky when the weather was cooler. My first thought was probably a solicitor of some kind. Fundraisers, replacement storm windows, pest control, we'd get all kinds of people offering services or goods in our neighborhood. I was not expecting to see two uniformed police officers when I opened the door.

One was a tall, white man with blond hair, looking every inch like Captain America. His partner was a Latina woman not much taller than five feet, with a round face and kind, brown eyes. "Hello, sir. Are you related to Kyle Thompson?" she asked.

"Yes, he's my husband," I said cautiously. "Can I help

you?" I had stolen a comic book from a local store when I was ten, but that was forty years ago. I couldn't think of anything that I had done recently that would warrant a police visit.

"I'm Officer Rodriguez, this is Officer Landin. May we come in?"

I frowned a little. Not that Kyle or I had anything to hide, but why would police officers want to come into our house? "Are you looking for something?"

Officer Landin's face remained stoic, but Officer Rodriguez gave me a gentle smile. "No, sir. We just need to talk to you."

I glanced back into the house, as if a mound of stolen weapons and drugs would appear in the middle of our coffee table, but it still looked as normal as ever. "Kyle is out, can it wait?"

"No." The single word from Officer Rodriguez instantly made my stomach drop. Something was wrong. Sweat broke out on my forehead and my hands as my body reacted to something my brain hadn't yet understood.

"Sure," I said, opening the door wider and stepping aside for them to enter.

They did, and then Officer Rodriguez gestured for me to sit in my recliner in the living room. I did but only perched on the edge of it, gazing nervously back at them. Officer Landin was doing his best impression of a marble statue, and Officer Rodriguez gave me a sad, kind smile. "You said Kyle Thompson is your husband? What is your name?"

"Yes," I said, leaning my elbows on my knees. "I'm Reuben Thompson. What is this about?"

Officer Rodriguez gave me a look that immediately made my stomach drop into my feet. "I'm afraid your husband is dead."

Six little words.

Six little words were all it took to shatter my world like a pane of glass.

"No," I said, much too quickly. "No, he just went out to pick up Chinese food. He'll be back in a few minutes."

Officer Landin shook his head once, his face still a mask of impassiveness. "No, Mr. Thompson. We're very sorry."

For some reason, I could feel every muscle in my body, and I realized I had a wide, dopey grin on my face. "No," I said again, shaking my head, which suddenly felt as heavy as if it were filled with concrete. "No, he just went out to grab dinner over at Jade Palace."

Officer Rodriguez gazed back at me, her warm, brown eyes full of what I recognized as pity. "We're so sorry, Mr. Thompson."

I think there's a moment when you get bad news where you're waiting for the punchline. For someone to pop up from behind the sofa and yell, "Surprise!", or to have some white guy with a microphone and camera step forward to tell you that it's all a trick, and you actually won a thousand dollars for playing along. I stared into the silence, waiting for the punchline. Whatever it was, it wasn't funny.

There was only silence except for a bleep of static from Officer Landin's radio on his shoulder, and he reached up to turn it down.

My eyes moved back and forth between the two police officers. The air around me suddenly felt like it was as thick as syrup, and I couldn't take a deep enough breath. There was no gotcha, no camera, no surprise. "What happened?" I heard the words come out of my mouth, but I could not remember forming them.

"There was an accident," Officer Rodriguez said, her voice low and what I assumed was meant to be calming. "That office building on Santos Street. We think one of the stone gargoyles must have broken. It fell while Mr. Thompson was walking underneath it."

I knew exactly what building she meant. We passed it almost every day. 'The Batman Building,' we would call it, because it looked like something out of Gotham, and, at night, covered in shadows where the streetlights didn't reach, the hulking, winged gargoyles looked like Batman crouched on the ledge, keeping his eye out for the evil villains of Gilmer Rock.

All of the air was gone from the room. My lungs felt like they compressed into tiny blocks. My head began to pound, and my eyes grew hot and heavy. The world went strangely silent, like I had suddenly been plunged under water, except for Officer Rodriguez's voice as she said, "We will need you, or someone who knew him, to come down to the morgue and identify him."

I started to shake. They were asking me to come look at Kyle's broken body. It would possibly be my last look at him. The last time I might get to see the man I had devoted my life to would be on a cold, metal table in a morgue. Of course, there was always the possibility that it wasn't him. That this was all just a huge misunderstanding, that some other poor soul had ended up beneath the fallen stone. My heart clung to the desperate hope that that was the case, even though I knew it was not. "Is... is that where he is right now?"

Officer Rodriguez hesitated. "He will be." My look of confusion must have prompted her, because she gently replied, "The crime scene investigators have to document the scene first."

I was able to read between the lines there. Kyle's body was still out on the street, because they needed to take photographs. Were people assembled even now, trying to look over the heads of the police to get a glimpse of him? Taking pictures and videos? Was there already social media commentary? I tried to rise from my chair, but my body felt as heavy as lead. "I... I need to see him."

Officer Rodriguez shook her head. "You don't want to see him like that," she said, her voice gentle but firm. "The morgue opens at 9am tomorrow morning."

I think I nodded, maybe I mumbled something in acknowledgement, I couldn't be sure I did either.

"Is there someone we can contact for you?" Officer

Landin said, his voice calm and steady, like a rumble of thunder. "Someone who can come be here with you?"

I wanted Kyle. He was the one who could comfort me. He was my rock, my foundation, my roots in a windstorm. And he was gone. "I... I don't know," I said.

"Family nearby? A neighbor?" Officer Rodriguez prompted.

I shook my head. Kyle was an only child and was estranged from his family. His parents had kicked him out at 17 when he had revealed that he was gay, and he had not spoken to either of them in over 30 years. They had not been invited to our wedding. Kyle didn't even have them as friends on his social media. My own mother had passed years ago, and my father was in his 80's with memory issues in assisted living several hours away. My younger sister, Brenda, was my closest relative, but even she was an hour and a half away, and she had 3 kids to look after. We weren't that close with any of our neighbors. At least, not close enough that I wanted any of them to come be with me.

"Do you want some coffee?" I asked suddenly. My momma would have beat my ass if I was an ungracious host. Here were two officers sitting in my living room, and I had not offered them anything.

The two exchanged glances with one another. "We're all right," Officer Landin said.

I nodded. "I need some coffee." I pushed myself to my feet. Why did my body feel so much heavier right now than it usually did?

"Can I help you?" Officer Rodriguez asked.

"No, no. You're a guest," I said, waving her down. "I'll be right back."

They let me exit to the kitchen, where two sets of dishes lay on our kitchen table, patiently waiting for Kyle to return with Chinese food. Chinese food that wasn't coming, because Kyle wasn't coming.

I stumbled, and the kitchen counter took my weight as I slumped against it, a sob tearing out of my lungs like I had been punched in the gut. Kyle was dead. The man I had loved since we had first met, who was supposed to grow old and gray with me, wasn't coming home ever again.

Officer Rodriguez followed after me, and she moved to my side to help me up. She must have been exceptionally strong despite her tiny frame, because she supported me easily as she led me over to the table, pulling out one of the chairs with her foot and easing me down into it. "I'm so sorry, Mr. Thompson. I know this is a terrible shock."

'Terrible shock' was putting it mildly. An asteroid could have been hurtling toward Earth right now, about to wipe out all of humanity, and I could not have cared less. I kept hearing a chant over and over in my head. *Kyle is dead. Kyle is dead. Kyle is dead...* On and on, like the droning of bees, blocking out everything else.

Officer Rodriguez pulled the paper napkin out from under one of the forks on the table and gave it to me to wipe my eyes and nose. My eyes felt swollen and squinty. I was sure I looked like an absolute mess. I blew my nose, only so I could try to breathe as sobs continued to wrack my frame. I could hear the soft crackle and garbled voice from Officer Landin's radio in the next room, and his cool, measured response, but the words were mush in my brain.

I must have cried for a good ten minutes, because the napkin was sopping wet by the time I stopped enough to take a deep breath and forced myself to get my breathing under control. The last thing I needed right now was to pass out and potentially fall or end up in the hospital. Officer Rodriguez knelt next to me, holding my hands as I cried. I wondered if she had had to do this before, been the one to break such horrible news to shocked families. She smiled gently and offered me another napkin, which I gratefully took. "Mr. Thompson, I'm so sorry for your loss. Is there someone we can call for you?"

I couldn't even think right now. Kyle had been my best friend, always there for me. There hadn't been a time since we got together in college that he had not been available as my support. Who did I even know? Who would I feel comfortable sharing this horrible tragedy with? I pulled my phone from my shorts pocket and began to sort through my contacts. So many contacts. So many encounters once in my life that had resulted in them being in my phone. Places like the customers service for an airline we had used back in our early 40's. Old high school and college friends that I hadn't spoken to in years. The dry cleaner's. A couple names that I couldn't place at the moment.

Finally, one name jumped out at me. Jacky McQueen, one of Kyle's fellow teachers who taught science. Jacky and her spouse Dex were some of the most outspoken queer people we knew in our area. Jacky was loud and bright and was the kind of person who made learning fun. Despite being nearly two decades younger than Kyle and I, she had become fast friends with Kyle when she started working at Gilmer Rock Middle School, and she and Dex would occasionally come over to our house to play board games and share a meal.

I looked up at Officer Rodriguez. "I... I think my friend Jacky and her spouse could come over."

Officer Rodriguez nodded slowly. "Do you need me to contact her for you?"

I shook my head. "I will."

Officer Rodriguez nodded again, giving my arm a reassuring squeeze. I was extremely grateful in this moment to have this absolute stranger by my side, making sure that I was not going through this alone. I hit the contact to call Jacky. I lifted the phone to my ear and listened to it ring. It felt almost unfamiliar; how often did we actually talk to our friends on the phone anymore instead of texting?

Jacky picked up after three rings. "Hello? Reuben?"

My mouth went dry. "Hi, Jacky," I croaked out. I didn't even recognize my own voice.

"Hi. What's up?"

"Um… Could you… come over? Kyle is dead."

There was a stunned silence on the other end of the phone before Jacky breathed, "Oh my god. What happened?"

What happened? It was a question that I had not been prepared for. And I didn't know how to answer. *He got smashed like a pancake by a falling gargoyle? Crushed by a stone monument in the middle of a busy street?* It sounded absurd in my own head. The sort of story you'd tell when you were making up a story to get a rise out of someone. Killed by escalator, decapitated by ceiling fan, grabbed by alligator. And, again, that feeling in my gut rose. If I said it out loud, it would be true.

"An… accident," I mumbled. That seemed a sufficient enough answer and the only coherent words I could form.

"Are you all right?" Of course I wasn't all right! I was in a million tiny shards on the kitchen floor. "Are you hurt?" Jacky asked, and I suddenly realized that my vague 'accident' explanation had probably implied to her that it was a car accident in which I was involved too.

"No, I'm… I'm not hurt. I wasn't… it was just him."

"Are you at home?" Jacky asked.

"Yes." I could at least answer that question without shaking.

"All right. Dex and I will be there shortly." Jacky hung up the phone.

I turned to Officer Rodriguez. "Our… our friend is coming over."

She nodded and gave me a small, sympathetic smile, one that I knew I was going to be tired of seeing very quickly. "Good. Officer Landin and I will stay here until they arrive, so you won't be alone."

The thought of being alone right now, even though I had been alone in the house only twenty minutes ago, was frightening. I supposed that's why they would stay with me, to ensure I was all right, that I wouldn't go running and screaming into the night or overdose on Tylenol in my sudden overwhelming shock and grief.

"What do I need to do?" I asked, my voice hoarse from crying.

Officer Rodriguez smiled and squeezed my hand. "Go to the morgue tomorrow morning to identify him. Officer Landin and I will also take a DNA sample tonight, which we will also use to confirm his identity."

"My DNA?" I asked, my brain not fully understanding the statement.

Officer Rodriguez thankfully kept a straight face. "No, sir. Something of your husband's. A comb or hairbrush, or a toothbrush? Something that was exclusively his."

Of course they wouldn't take my DNA to identify Kyle. I knew it was the trauma making me unable to think clearly, but I still felt a little ridiculous. "After that?"

"You can arrange with a funeral home to take care of him after the medical examiner releases the body," Officer Rodriguez said.

I nodded numbly. I would have to take care of all of that, when we should have been planning something fun, like our upcoming fishing trip.

Officer Landin appeared in the doorway, giving me a small, polite smile. "I'm sorry to bother you, Mr. Thompson, but do you have something of your husband's that we could take for DNA analysis?"

I nodded, pushing myself unsteadily to my feet and heading for the stairs. There were 14 steps total, but each one felt like climbing a mountain with no oxygen. I made my way into our bedroom, then the bathroom, grabbing Kyle's blue and white toothbrush from where it sat on the counter. Not like he was going to need it again. I brought it back downstairs, and Officer Landin tucked it carefully into an evidence bag. "Thank you. Do you want it back after we've gotten a DNA sample?"

I shook my head. "No." Even my addled brain knew I wasn't going to use Kyle's toothbrush myself.

We sat back down in the living room. There was silence between us now except for the occasional crackle of the police radios. I found myself leaning my elbows on my knees, my face in my hands, as I tried to process the situation. Everything was quiet until there was the sound of car doors closing outside, and then a knock on the door before Jacky and Dex walked in. Jacky was in her early 30's, with brown hair pulled up into a messy bun held in place with a mechanical pencil. Behind her came her spouse, Dex, whose short hair was bleached blond, setting off their tanned skin. Jacky hurried into the living room, moving over to wrap her arms around me and hug me tightly. "Oh, Reuben, I'm so sorry," she moaned.

I accepted her hug, then another one as she stood and Dex took her place. Jacky turned to the officers. "I'm Jacky McQueen, I work at Gilmer Rock Middle School with Kyle."

Officer Rodriguez bobbed her head. "Officer Rodriguez, my partner, Officer Landin. Thank you for coming."

Jacky stepped closer to them, and their voices dropped away as I just sat in my chair, Dex holding me close. They smelled like coconut and acrylic paint. After a few minutes, the officers turned to me. "We're going to head out, unless there is anything else you need at the moment, Mr. Thompson."

I lifted my head, my eyes stinging, my cheeks puffy. I was sure I looked about as horrible as I ever had in my life. "No, thank you. I'll go to the morgue tomorrow." I tried to smile, but my face felt stiff with salt, and I wasn't sure if I would be able to summon a smile ever again.

The two officers headed out, and I heard them get into their car as Jacky turned to me. "Fuck, Ruby. I'm so sorry. What can we do?"

I shook my head. I had no idea. I only knew that I didn't want to be alone. My stomach let out a growl. "Did you eat dinner?" Jacky asked.

I shook my head again. "No. Kyle was… on his way to grab Jade Palace. But I'm not hungry."

"I know, but you have to eat something," Jacky wheedled.

"How about some toast, at least?" Dex asked. I nodded, just because I knew it would make them happy. Dex got up and vanished into the kitchen.

Jacky sat down on the floor in front of me and rubbed my knees with her hands. "Hey, it's okay. We'll help you sort this out."

"Thank you," I mumbled.

"We should probably call Madelaine," Jacky ventured gently. Madelaine O'Dillon was the principal at Gilmer Rock Middle School where Kyle taught English. If anyone needed to know, it was Madelaine. The kids wouldn't have Mr. Thompson in class tomorrow. I was grateful for Jacky being able to think right now. I pulled out my phone. My hands were shaking, but I didn't feel it. I didn't feel anything except cold. A numbing cold that seeped deep under my skin and into the marrow of my bones, leeching warmth and happiness from me. I scrolled through my contacts, names rapidly flicking by, and I realized none of them knew yet. None of these hundreds of contacts in my phone list knew that my life had just been smashed apart. I was going to have to tell them. Which meant that I would have to acknowledge the truth, that Kyle was gone. I skimmed my list of contacts, names flying past, meaningless, a jumble of letters that equated a link to someone. A piece of my life, some of them long-forgotten. Old college friends I hadn't talked to in twenty plus years, clients from when I worked in sales, my current co-workers, my boss. Seeing that name made me freeze for a moment. I would have to tell my boss. I still had a job. How was I supposed to get up in the morning, let alone put on a suit and drive in to the office building and crunch numbers, without Kyle there?

I couldn't find Madelaine's number. I thought I had it, but apparently, I didn't. The school's office line wouldn't be monitored this late in the evening. "I don't have her number."

Jacky pulled out her own phone with the information. I punched the numbers into my phone with unsteady hands before holding it to my ear again. The ringing echoed inside of my head like my brain had disappeared, leaving my skull a hollow cavern of nothingness. I had a pounding headache forming, and I knew I needed to drink something and take something for my head. But lifting my body out of my chair felt like a Herculean task. So, I sat, and I counted the rings. Maybe Madelaine wouldn't pick up. The fourth ring had almost completed when the phone clicked. "Hello, Madelaine speaking," she said in her no-nonsense tone.

"H... Hi," I said, suddenly realizing I had very little breath, and my voice came out high and shaky.

"Hello. Who is this?" Madelaine's voice was calm but strong. She sounded very much like the principal she was.

"Madelaine, hi, it... it's Reuben Thompson. Kyle's

husband." I forced the words out in one big breath that left my lungs aching and starved for oxygen.

"Oh, yes, hello, Mr. Thompson," Madelaine said, all business. "How are you?"

The pleasantry caught me off guard, and I realized I had no words again. How was I? I was cold. I was numb. I was angry. I was scared. I was sad. I was so many things, stuffed inside an empty shell filled with nothing yet weighing a million pounds. "Good," I heard myself say. A fucking automatic response to a generic platitude. I was not 'good.' I was anything but 'good.' But that had been the only word that I could summon from the depths of my brain.

There was silence on the other end, and I realized Madelaine was probably waiting for me to say something. It would have been polite to ask how she was, but honestly, I didn't care. Why would I care how she was? She was alive, and probably at home with whatever family she had, safe and warm and whole.

"May I help you with something?" she asked after what must have been a very long moment of silence. Her voice was pleasant but still no-nonsense, a patient adult to a misbehaving student. I turned my eyes to Jacky, and she gave me an encouraging smile.

I wasn't sure if I would be able to speak, but I knew I had to. "I... I'm sorry to tell you this, but Kyle passed away tonight."

It was her turn to be silent on the other end of the phone.

I wondered what she was thinking. If she gripped her phone a little tighter, if her stomach dropped like mine had, if her vision became a blur.

"My god," she finally said, letting out a soft breath. "I... I'm so sorry. What happened?"

"There was an accident. A construction accident." Yes, that sounded more appropriate. Less like a car crash, and more like the act of nature that it was.

"Oh, I'm so sorry," Madelaine said, and she genuinely did sound sorry, her normally brusque voice breathy and higher than usual.

"I just figured you should know," I said, as if that wasn't obvious to both of us. "For his classes and everything."

"Yes, of course, we'll take care of all of that. And I'm sure there will be some paperwork for you, and his personal affects in his classroom."

That thought made my lungs squeeze again in my chest. There would be paperwork. Lots of paperwork. And Kyle's belongings. They would have to be gone through. My head swam, and Madelaine's words became no more than a buzz in my head. And then there was silence. I realized she had asked me a question. "What?" I murmured.

"I asked if there will be a funeral," Madelaine said. "I'm sure the staff and his students would like to attend."

Another thing to think about. A funeral. Flowers. A casket, if he could even have one of those. A service. A headstone. A grave somewhere. A reception afterwards.

Food. Having to listen to dozens, maybe even hundreds, of people say his name over and over again, come up to me, hug me, tell me how sorry they were. There was so much to think about, and I didn't want to think about any of it. Not right now. "I'll let you know," I mumbled numbly.

"Yes, of course," Madelaine said. "Well, I am here if you need anything. We'll get everything figured out."

"Okay," I mumbled into the phone. "Goodbye." I hung up the phone and set it on the arm of the chair. *Everything figured out.* Like navigating this tragedy was just a puzzle in the Sunday paper. Solve the riddle, and Kyle would come back. I suddenly understood those movies and TV shows, where the hero lost their loved one and would do anything to get them back. Where even their own death could not stop them; they'd rise from the grave years or centuries in the future to find their lost love. I felt that in my bones. If someone had said to me in that moment that if I went forward in time and fought giant space monsters for a chance at a magic spell that would bring Kyle back right then, I would have done it, damn the consequences.

Dex came back out with a plate of toast and a large glass of ice water. My stomach churned at the thought of eating anything, but I knew I had to take care of myself. I swallowed the ice water, the cold making my headache worse, and then I took a piece of the buttered toast, chewing mechanically and swallowing it without tasting it.

My phone rang where it sat on the arm of the chair. It

was Jade Palace. They were probably calling to see if we were going to pick up the food we had ordered. It rang and rang, feeling endless. But I couldn't answer. If I picked up that phone and told the person on the other end that Kyle was dead, it would become real. If I said the words out loud, that meant they were true.

Jacky glanced at it, then at me. "Want me to answer?" she asked.

I shook my head, and we all went quiet again until the phone stopped ringing. I wondered if they had tried calling Kyle's phone first. I wondered if his phone had even survived the accident. If it had, hopefully I could get it back. There were things on there I might need. His email, his social media, his fellow teachers and other contacts. I knew all the pieces of Kyle, but now I was going to have to find a way to wrap them up into a neat little package, to be placed on a shelf.

"Is there something we can do for you right now?" Jacky asked. "Make some calls? Draw you a bath?"

"I think I just want to lie down," I said softly. Maybe if I laid down, I would wake up to find this was all just a bad dream.

Jacky nodded. "All right, honey."

As I curled up in our bed, I hugged Kyle's pillow to my chest. It was cool and didn't smell like him the way that people often said pillows did in novels. It smelled like a pillow, and it did nothing to ease the ache deep inside of me.

But I still clung to it, shedding tears into it until I felt more wrung out than a dishcloth. I finally fell asleep. When I woke up again later that night, I was still all alone in bed.

Chapter 2

Reuben

I DIDN'T WANT TO go to the morgue the next morning, but I knew I had to. I forced myself to take a shower and shove more toast in my mouth, about the only thing I could manage to prepare. I had a splitting headache, so I chugged some meds and too much coffee. I realized I had forgotten to tell my manager at the bank what had happened. I could not bring myself to talk to him on the phone, so I sent a simple text.

My husband passed away yesterday. I need a few days off. Will call later. I did not get a response right away, but that was fine. I just needed to get this horrible first morning over with. So, I got in my car and drove to the Gilmer Rock Morgue.

Dex met me there. Jacky had to teach her classes, but Dex

was an artist who worked from home, so they could be more flexible. They smiled at me, the movement tight. I could feel the apology on their face. "Ready?"

"No," I said, shaking my head, but I still pushed past them and into the single-story building. Walking in, the smell was unlike anything I had known before. The antiseptic odor of a hospital, the strange sort of powdery perfume smell that I associated with senior ladies, something a little too sweet that I couldn't identify. It almost made me gag. I fought down the feeling, taking a deep breath through my mouth before heading further inside, Dex following after me, the hum of fluorescent lights overhead like the drone of swarming flies.

The front office looked like a doctor's office, with a desk and plastic chairs in a small waiting area. The woman behind the desk had graying chestnut curls pinned up in an attempt at an updo that looked like it was trying to escape from her head. She had black framed cat-eye glasses, and she wore a shade of fuchsia lipstick that was not doing her skin tone any favors.

"Can I help you?" she asked in the pleasant tone of an office worker who didn't want to be there. She had lipstick on her top teeth.

"Hi, I'm Reuben Thompson," I said slowly.

She gazed back at me, facial features not changing. Why had I thought that she would recognize my name? She probably didn't know the name of any of the corpses back beyond those heavy metal doors. They didn't mean anything to her, even though one of them meant everything to me.

"I'm here to… My husband… Kyle… last night." I was fumbling for the words I still hadn't been able to figure out how to say out loud.

"Are you here to identify a deceased?" she asked with almost no inflection to her tone.

"Yes," I said, my fingers clinging to the edge of the counter so tightly that they were turning white.

The woman turned to her computer that looked like it was from the days of dial-up, typing something into it. The clack of the keys was oddly loud in the almost unnatural stillness of the place. After a moment, she turned back to me and nodded her head toward the small bank of chairs. "Have a seat. The medical examiner will be with you shortly."

"Thank you." It felt important to be polite, even if this woman looked like she would rather be getting a colonoscopy than sitting behind that desk. I moved over to a chair, sitting down gingerly on it. Dex perched on a seat next to me. How many people had sat in these unforgiving, uncomfortable chairs on the worst day of their lives? I was sure the number had to be hundreds, maybe thousands. I folded my hands on my knees as I leaned on them, my foot bouncing mechanically without me realizing it. My phone buzzed in my pocket, but I ignored it. I didn't feel like talking to anyone right now, and the stillness of the room felt like it shouldn't be breached with something as mundane as a phone call.

Dex rested a hand on my arm, their black-painted nails chipped. "Doing okay?" they asked.

"Yeah." I didn't know what else to say. Of course I wasn't doing okay.

A man with fuzzy, gray hair, wearing mint green scrubs and a white lab coat stepped out of the door and glanced toward us. "Mr. Thompson?"

I stood up too fast, my vision swimming, and I had to lean against Dex for a moment. They took it in stride, at least. "Yes, that's me."

The gray-haired man nodded and gave me a sympathetic smile that I was becoming all too familiar with. "I'm Doctor Morton, the medical examiner for the county. Would you please come back with me?"

Dex and I followed him. He held open the metal door, then stepped in front of us to lead us down a long hallway. "Who are you here to identify?"

I swallowed hard, trying to force words out, but the sickly-sweet air had stolen my voice. Dr. Morton turned back to me, waiting. I glanced at Dex, who, thankfully, jumped in. "His husband, Kyle Thompson. He was... in an accident last night."

"Oh, yes," Dr. Morton said, giving me another sympathetic look. "We have Mr. Thompson's body covered right now. You can identify him in the room, or if you'd prefer it, you can look through the viewing window."

That confused me, as the few times I had seen body

identification on TV, the person was usually right next to the corpse on the table. For a moment, I thought maybe that would be best, just seeing him from a distance, like a television screen. But the thought of not being right next to him when he needed me most (as irrational as I knew that was) tugged at my heart, and I knew I'd regret it if I put that distance between us.

"I'd like to see him in person," I gulped out, the words coming out a strange mix of both too loud and too quiet.

Dr. Morton nodded silently before he pushed open the swinging double doors to a room with bright overhead lights. An orderly in a set of scrubs was in the corner, glancing up at us, then going back to whatever he was doing. There was a body lying on a gurney nearby, covered head to toe with a blue medical drape. At least, I knew it must be a body, based on the general shape of it, but parts of it looked wrong. I couldn't tell exactly what with the draping, but what should have been various raised parts of a person were not raised. I could make out feet at one end, but at the other end where there should have been shoulders and a head, the shape was odd. My stomach lurched, and I prayed to any deities that existed that I was not about to throw up. "Let me prepare you, Mr. Thompson," Dr. Morton said, his word a little softer and calming. "There was a lot of damage done by the stone that fell. It landed nearly directly on top of him. His brain stem, here," he lifted his hand to touch the back of his own head, "that controls bodily functions like breathing and other senses was impacted almost immediately."

"What does that mean?" I asked. I thought I knew, but my own brain was still trying to catch up to the situation, and it was also working to suppress my surging stomach.

Dr. Morton's smile was kind and also knowing. "It very likely was an instant death. He probably didn't feel a thing."

I wasn't sure if this man was lying to me about that or not, but either way, I was grateful for the answer. If I had known that Kyle was frightened and in pain before he died, I knew that idea would haunt me.

"But because of that, the stone also did some very severe damage to his head. You don't have to look at his face. And, to be honest, I wouldn't recommend that you do."

A weird feeling settled over me at that. I had been preparing myself that the last sight I might see of the man I had loved for so many years would be some sort of crushed, bloody mess. "But I need to look at him to identify him?"

Dr. Morton nodded. "Yes. It helps us to confirm the identity so we can move forward while we wait on the DNA confirmation." I remembered Officer Landin taking Kyle's toothbrush the evening before. "But you don't have to look at his face to identify him. Tell me, does your husband have any identifying marks on his body? Scars, perhaps from surgery or old injury? Tattoos? Piercings?"

I shook my head. Neither of us had tattoos. I was trying to think of something else that could identify him. "Birth marks or defects?" Dr. Morton prompted. "Freckles or moles? Distinctive features you would recognize?"

"Kyle has a dark freckle on the inside of his left forearm," I said. "And... his little toe on his right foot is deformed from when he broke it as a child."

Dr. Morton nodded. I half expected him to just whip off the sheet entirely, like a magician doing a gruesome magic trick, but instead he only moved around to Kyle's right side and folded up the sheet for me to see the bare right foot. The small toe was crooked, the area around the nailbed starting to turn an unnatural blue color. Dr. Morton watched my face, and when he saw the devastation cross it, he covered the foot and moved around to the left side of the gurney. He folded back part of the blue sheet, just enough to see Kyle's arm. It was unclothed, and there was blood spattered in several places, as well as other abrasions to his skin, which was not its usual color. There was a gray tinge to it. Dr. Morton lifted the limp arm, holding it surprisingly gently, as if he were manipulating a broken limb rather than a dead one. He turned the arm slightly so I could see. There was the freckle, so familiar, yet suddenly so foreign. I knew that was him. Any lingering hopes I had had that a mistake had been made, that Kyle had disappeared and would reappear suddenly with a story to tell of aliens or mafia kidnappers, was gone. "Yes," I said. "That's Kyle."

Dr. Morton nodded and set the arm down on the steel table again with as soft a sound as he could. The left hand was limp and mottled with discoloration, and there was an indentation where his wedding ring had been, but it was not there now.

"Where is his ring?" I asked, my thumb automatically moving to my own gold band on my left hand and giving it a stroke. I had worn it for so long, it felt like a part of me now.

"We removed it, along with his clothing and assets," Dr. Morton said. "You will get all of it back after we release his body."

"Release?" I asked, suddenly picturing myself having to carry Kyle out of the morgue like a mummy and stick him in the trunk of my car.

"To the mortuary," Dr. Morton said. "If you want to make arrangements at a specific location, you can let the officers in charge of his case know. They will communicate that to us, and we will have them pick up the body once our autopsy is concluded. His personal things will go with him; the funeral director will be able to give them back to you."

I nodded numbly. One more thing to think about when all my body wanted to do was fold in on itself and never get up again. "Can I... have a few minutes alone with him?"

Dr. Morton gave me another sympathetic smile. "I'm afraid I can't leave you alone with the body, per protocol. But I can certainly step away to give you as much privacy as I can."

It was going to have to do if I wanted to say goodbye to the man I had been with for the majority of my life. I turned helpless eyes to Dex. "Um..."

Dex gave me a nod. "I can wait in the lobby. Take all the time you need." They turned and headed back out the swinging doors.

Dr. Morton gave me another smile and moved over to a nearby desk, doing his best impression of ignoring me. The orderly was still busy doing God only knows what in the corner of the room, still not paying attention to me either. I took the left hand that Dr. Morton had uncovered; it was startlingly cold and heavy. I supposed that was what the term 'deadweight' referred to. Funny how that had never occurred to me until now. It was Kyle's hand; I could feel the familiar bones and lines and ridges of the hand I had held so many times. But it felt unnatural. Cold and stiff, inflexible. Not at all like the warm, vivacious, child-loving teacher I had known for over half of my life.

I wanted to see his face. I wanted to know that this was the man I had married. It was devastating that I had to make an identification of someone I loved so dearly from a few pieces of skin. But this wasn't a forensic drama, with a pretty corpse spread on the table, with makeup to make them look dead but not uncomfortably so. If the doctor had covered his face and suggested I not look at it to identify him, I felt that I had to respect his expertise. But I still could not stop myself from lifting up the edge of the blue sheet near his head until I could see a little bit of skin. If it could even be called that. What I could see looked more like raw hamburger meat mashed together. I knew I had to be looking at the side of his neck, but it looked like nothing I could recognize. I quickly dropped the sheet back in place. My imagination ran wild enough; it was better to remember him as he was when he was alive.

I put my hands gently onto the area of his torso. He was curled a little, and I could feel that some of the bones and things beneath the skin did not feel like they were supposed to. Even without the warmth and tension that a living body had, this didn't feel like a human form. I was sure that Dr. Morton could tell me exactly what happened in medical terms, but I didn't need to know. I didn't want to know. I didn't need the precise details to know that I was not going to get my husband back.

I went back to holding his hand, running my thumb over where his ring no longer sat. I could see and feel the indentation of it, and I just kept stroking that. My tongue was heavy in my mouth. My head was full of everything and nothing. There were so many things I wanted to say, but I also realized that it didn't matter. Kyle was gone; if the afterlife existed and he could hear me, he could hear me whether I said it now or later. I didn't know what to say or how to say it in this cold, unfeeling room, surrounded by strangers. But I also would not get to hold his hand ever again. I might not even see him again, the little I could see of him now. Even though we had been together for over 25 years, I still found myself studying the marks on his skin as if I had never seen them before. Wrinkles and tiny freckles and the indentations of his nail beds suddenly became the most important thing for me to look at. I had to memorize every little piece of him. It had only been overnight, but I felt like I was already starting to forget. The sound of his voice, his laugh, the feel of his arms around me, his lips kissing my ear.

The room was cold, and the hand I held was cold, and my body felt like I might never be warm again. Like I could just curl up on the table next to him and freeze to death. I knew I couldn't just stand there forever. Dr. Morton had work to do, and I did too. I had... My mind was blank. There was probably so much I needed to do, and I could think of none of it. I ran my thumb again over where his wedding ring had been removed. The funeral director would give it back to me. Yes, that was what I needed to do now. I needed to arrange his funeral.

I lifted his heavy hand to my lips and pressed a gentle kiss to the back of it. It would have to be enough. "Thank you," I said to Dr. Morton, my voice husky as tears threatened to blind me.

Dr. Morton nodded and gave me a kind smile. I turned and left the icy room with its scent of chemicals and death, back to the lobby where Dex waited.

They smiled at me when I appeared, the same smile Dr. Morton had given me. I had a feeling I was going to see that smile a lot. Dex led me out into the sunshine, which at least made me feel less like I was standing in a walk-in freezer. My hands were shaking, and I told myself it was from the cold.

"What do you need me to do?" Dex asked gently.

"I... I don't know," I said slowly. "I need to find a funeral home, I guess."

Dex patted my shoulder. "Do you need help with that?"

I shook my head. That seemed like it might be a little too personal to involve Dex, and by extension, Jacky. "I'll take care of it. After I talk to them, I'll let you know?"

Dex nodded. "All right, Ruby. I'll be at home if and when you need anything."

"Thank you," I said automatically. Dex got into their car and drove off, leaving me standing alone in front of the morgue. I tipped my face up toward the sunshine, the warmth spreading over my skin as tears began to fall. I quickly made my way to my car and closed myself inside before I burst into wracking sobs that shook me to my core.

They only lasted for a minute, which I was grateful for. I wiped my face on my sleeve, as I didn't have anything else to clear it with, before I pulled out my phone. I had several text messages from various people, expressing their condolences and asking if there was anything they could do. I ignored most of them, not feeling like I could focus on other people right now. My boss from the bank had texted too, with the same platitudes, but at least he also granted me as much time away as I needed.

I googled funeral homes near me. When my mother had passed away from breast cancer, it had been a slow enough decline that she and my father had been able to make arrangements in advance. I had no first-hand knowledge on what to do. I just wanted it to be easy and over as soon as possible. The first place I called did not pick up the phone, so I tried the second one. A warm, soft female voice answered, "Blue Skies Funeral Home, this is Carol, how can I help you?"

My breath caught, and I swallowed hard. "Hi, Carol. Uh, my name's Reuben. Would you... be available to do a funeral for my husband?" I wasn't sure if that was the correct way to go about asking or not, but the woman on the other end didn't seem concerned.

"I'm so sorry," she said, sounding genuinely remorseful. "Is he already passed?"

"Yes," I said. "He's at the Gilmer Rock Morgue."

"Yes, we can absolutely take care of that for you," Carol replied. "Do you have time to come in today for a consultation?"

A few questions and minutes later, I had an appointment for that afternoon to meet with Mr. Greenley at Blue Skies Funeral Home. I drove myself home and then stood under the shower until the water went cold before I got out again and made myself some eggs for lunch. I figured I better use them before they went bad, since only one of us was in the house to eat them.

The meeting with the funeral director, Marvin Greenley, seemed to take forever, yet it passed in a blur. Marvin ran the mortuary with his family, Carol being his wife. I was extremely grateful for him and his son Calvin who joined us. My heart was set at ease when I met Calvin and found out that he was trans, and Marvin and Carol supported him fully. Even in places as accepting as Gilmer Rock, there were still plenty of people who hated people based on their skin color or their sexual orientation. Calvin reminded me of Kyle in his younger years, enthusiastic and a bit flamboyant, but also very empathetic and comforting. If he was not helping his father run the mortuary, I thought he might make a very good teacher.

There were many decisions that had to be made, more than I would have ever thought about on my own. "Remember, while the departed person is the reason for the gathering, the loved ones are who the funeral is for," Marvin told me. "Don't only choose things that Kyle would have liked. Choose things that are comforting to you as well."

With his and Calvin's help, and a plate of cookies and homemade lemonade from Carol, we made arrangements for the coming Tuesday. When I told Marvin about the accident that took Kyle, Marvin thought cremation would be better than a closed casket, and I agreed. He also gave me a checklist of things they needed from me and things that I needed to do, which I knew was going to be very helpful. My mind was still on a roller coaster, with sharp turns, sudden drops, and sluggish climbs. Until the death certificates arrived, my ability to do paperwork would be limited, so I focused on the immediate needs of the funeral.

Blue Skies had a room large enough for a service with about eighty attendees, which seemed like plenty of space. Marvin and Carol had provided me with a list of locations they often partnered with for things like catering and flowers. I didn't want to think too hard, so I just called the first ones on the list and went with what they recommended. Kyle was the sort of person who would research all of the options and then make a list of pros and cons. I could be that person when I wanted to be, but right now, all I wanted was for things to be simple. Making any decision at all felt like trying to jump over a canyon. My financial analyst brain at least kept a running track of the expenses, and I counted myself once again lucky that it was not a huge concern with how I would pay for the funeral. We weren't rich, by any means, especially with Kyle's teacher salary, but we were comfortable and had some savings built up. I also figured Kyle's life insurance would pay out at some point, as if a lump sum of money could make up for all of the years we would no longer have together. That was another place I would have to contact, and I added it to my rapidly-growing list.

Chapter 3

Reuben

Carol called me the next day, which was Saturday, and asked if I wanted to come pick up Kyle's personal affects; his body had been delivered to the mortuary that morning, and they were planning to cremate him that afternoon. It was a good excuse for me to get out of the house that felt as empty as if I had never lived there. The sun was bright, almost too bright. The world was continuing to spin, even as my own world had ground to a staggering halt.

I drove to Blue Skies with my window down. As I stopped at a red light, the sound of laughter from the sidewalk nearby caught my attention. A young couple were standing in front of a restaurant and posing for a selfie with a phone. My heart ached. They looked so happy. They probably had decades together ahead of them. Or, maybe they didn't. Maybe tonight the young man would have an allergic reaction to shellfish, or the woman would fall down a flight of steps. Happiness was only guaranteed for the moment. At any time, a stray bullet could come flying, or a car could jump the curb, or a decorative stone could fall off of a building. I brooded over the unknown future of these two strangers, the king of death, a grim reaper seeing only darkness, my mind lost in a black swirl of despair.

A horn blared at me, making me jump, and I realized the light had turned green while I had been lost in thought. I gave the guy behind me a quick wave and hurried through the intersection, keeping my eyes focused on the road. The last thing I needed right now was to get into an accident. As tempting as it was to think about turning the wheel and just smashing into a building or something, I couldn't let those dark, intrusive thoughts take over.

I parked at the funeral home and went in. It was cool inside, the air conditioner making the air a stark contrast from outside. And there was a smell to the place, I realized. I hadn't noticed it yesterday. But today, it felt like it was assaulting my senses, thick and cloying in my throat. Flowers and chemicals and something else. Did sorrow have a smell? If it did, I was sure this was it. I coughed into my elbow, tears forming in my eyes, though whether from the smell or the emotions racing through me, I had no idea.

Calvin, the son, was sitting at the desk inside the office area and looked up as I stood in the entryway. He smiled at me, the small, sympathetic smile I was rapidly growing accustomed to. "Hello, Mr. Thompson," he said politely, waving me into the office.

The office still had the same sickly-sweet smell to it as I sat. There was a bowl of peppermints on the desk in front of me. I took one and popped it into my mouth, letting the cool bite take over my senses. Calvin gave me a knowing look before he reached beneath the desk. He pulled up two paper grocery bags, setting them on the desk.

"This one has Kyle's personal affects," he said gently, motioning to one. "There's a card on the front listing all of them." He nodded at the other one. "These are his clothes that were taken off of him at the morgue, but I have to warn you, they're pretty... unpleasant. If you want them, you can have them, but otherwise, I can put them in with him to be cremated."

I took the first bag, sucking on the peppermint in my mouth as I scanned down the inventory list. On it was his cell phone, a chapstick, a pen, his wallet and everything that was in it down to the last penny and reward card, and his wedding ring. I glanced quickly inside to confirm it was all there before turning to Calvin again. Another person whose expertise it would be best to trust in this matter, I figured. "Yes, if that could go with him," I said, nodding my head at the other bag. I didn't want to see his bloody clothing; that was not a memory I needed. "Thank you. I really appreciate it."

Calvin quickly took the bag and set it back down out of sight behind the desk. "You're welcome, Mr. Thompson. Is there anything else I can do for you right now, or any questions I can answer?"

"No," I said, crunching the peppermint in my mouth. The crack of it sounded like the snap of a whip in the quiet space. "Thank you, the lists you gave me have been very helpful."

"Good," Calvin said, seeming to perk up a little at that. "It's so hard dealing with death, especially when it happens so suddenly. I think having the information readily available really makes a difference."

"It does," I said, hugging the paper bag to my chest.

When I got home, I pulled the items out of the bag one by one and laid them out. The items were so familiar, yet so foreign at the same time. They were the things that Kyle had used daily, and I could see all of the little wear patterns on them. The leather slick and shiny on his wallet where it had slid in and out of his pocket so many times. The place where the writing on the side of the pen had been rubbed away from where he held it. The chapstick nearly gone in its little tube. I picked up his cell phone. One corner had a pretty good spider-web of a crack in it, but most of the screen was relatively unblemished. I noticed that the screen looked like it had been cleaned recently. I wondered if there had been blood on it before it was returned to me.

I tried to turn it on, but the battery was dead. I would have to plug it in. Posting on social media would be the easiest way to reach the people who needed to know, though that seemed like a terrible way for people to find out someone they knew had died. But I couldn't bear the thought of having to call so many people, many of whom I did not know well, and have the same conversation over and over again. So, I posted on my own social media, trying to strike the right balance between too much information and not enough. I posted on Kyle's profiles too, and then I did my best to set my phone aside. I was getting notifications left and right, but I knew that most of them would all be the same thing. So sorry for your loss, lots of love, let me know if you need anything. It was all too mind-numbing, and I didn't want to think about it anymore.

The days leading up to the funeral were a blur. I know Dex and Jacky came over several times, always bringing food with them, whether it was fast food or something homemade. Information for the funeral was sent out via email and social media. On Monday night, the night before the funeral, Jacky brought over a box filled with homemade cards from Kyle's students. Some of them had stories about Mr. Thompson in them, some of them had sketches in various levels of talent, lots of them had hearts and tear drops drawn on them.

It warmed me inside to see so much love expressed for

Kyle from his students, who were everything to him. We had never had kids of our own, a lot of it having to do with prejudice against gay couples. But Kyle worked at the school, and I volunteered with local programs that worked with at-risk youth, so we knew we were making a difference, even a small one, in the lives of each child we worked with. It still ended up surprising me when I came to the mortuary on Tuesday, and they had to add standing room out into the vestibule for Kyle's funeral.

The funeral was led by a local minister, Pastor Jones, that I had known from some of the youth programs I volunteered with. We kept the service simple. Pastor Jones had asked if I wanted to speak at the funeral, but I had declined. I had never been good at public speaking, and I knew I would not hold it together if I did. Jacky got up and read through the biography of Kyle's life that she and I had written out, especially touching on how much Kyle had meant to his students. Then Pastor Jones invited people to come up front and say a few words about Kyle if they wanted to. Several of his teacher friends and two current students came up and shared sweet stories.

The rest of that day went by in a blink. It was a flurry of handshakes, hugs, small smiles, soft voices. Each of Kyle's students came up to me to say how sorry they were and that they would miss Mr. Thompson. Several of them were crying, and I had a big wet spot on the front of my suit jacket by the time all of them had come through. We ate a meal prepared by the catering company I hired, which I barely tasted. And then it was time to go home. Jacky and Dex brought a box of cards out to my car, and I carried the urn with Kyle's ashes and a small flower arrangement in my arms. I fastened them both into the passenger seat of my car. The urn looked so small. How could a man with so much life and love fit into such a small container? The human body really was made up of hardly anything.

And that was it. I was alone. The funeral was done. I had gone from a lifeboat with a few steady hands to assist to suddenly being adrift on the water with no help in sight. What did I need to do? There were places that needed to be contacted, no doubt plenty of paperwork to fill out. The world continued its spin around the solar system while I stood numbly in place, my own world crumbling like a sand castle under a wave. There would probably be a few check-ins for a few days from people, but even those would fall off.

I don't remember driving home, but I must have, because I found myself sitting on the floor of my living room, my suit jacket tossed over the couch, sorting through the cards from the funeral. More paper to deal with. I was completely wrung out. I wanted to cry, but I couldn't even summon the energy for that anymore. I had cried more in the last few days than I had my entire life. I didn't even think it was possible to cry that much. And now, I couldn't. I was too exhausted. The thought of doing anything other than sitting on the floor felt like trying to scale a mountain. I sat there for hours until the sunlight started to fade, and the room darkened. I carried Kyle's urn upstairs to our bedroom and put him on the nightstand next to me, because I didn't know where else to put him. "Good night, sweetie," I said softly to it as I settled into the cold, lonely sheets. Silence was the only reply.

Chapter 4

Reuben

THE DAY AFTER THE funeral, I had a pounding headache from crying and not hydrating enough. Kyle would always scold me for being a camel and not drinking enough water. I took a long, hot shower, ate some food, took something for my head, and then sat down at Kyle's laptop on the folding table in the living room. I had decided to take the rest of the week off to try to sort through Kyle's affairs, a task that I knew I'd have to face sooner rather than later.

Sorting through Kyle's personal email was interesting. Years and years of purchases were reflected back at me from the massive number of assorted companies and products that emailed him. There were a few emails recently from people he knew, sending their condolences, though why they sent them to Kyle's personal email, I had no idea. I deleted most of the junk, and I responded to a few of the well-wishers and those who didn't seem to know that Kyle had passed away. Former students, parents of students, old friends he hadn't talked to in years. It was all sort of a jumbled mess. I wondered if after this I could just never open his email again and let all of the junk go into some sort of nebulous spam graveyard.

And then I saw an email notification from Monster Match, stating that he had received a new message in his chat with someone named *SeaKing Swimmer*. My mind drifted back to the conversations Kyle and I had had months before.

"What do you want to do for your birthday?" Kyle asked me as we ate dinner. We had celebrated my 50th birthday last year with a big party with our friends and family at a local event space, and we would probably do the same when Kyle turned 50 later this year. But for 51, I didn't plan to do a large party again, or any sort of gathering. I was perfectly happy to spend the time with Kyle, doing something fun together.

"I don't know," I said. "I'm open to suggestions."

"You mentioned a few years ago that you had never been fishing before," Kyle said. "Would you maybe want to do that? Rent one of those fancy boat things, go out on the ocean for a few days, do some deep-sea fishing?"

"Sure!" I replied. Despite living so close to both a lake and an ocean, I had never gone fishing before. The closest thing I had gotten to either of them was swim lessons as a kid at the local

community center, and an occasional jaunt in a swimming pool. But even recently, that had been few and far between; adults just generally didn't go swimming that often, it seemed. But fishing could be fun, even if we didn't catch anything. Being able to sit on the ocean, surrounded by nothing but water for miles, just Kyle and I, side by side, talking and laughing, sounded like a little slice of Heaven.

We had encountered many monsters in our town of Gilmer Rock over the recent years. The school Kyle worked at offered tutoring and lectures on various subjects throughout the year, aimed at helping educate the new monster visitors, though human community members often joined as well. Many of the monsters were strange, colorful creatures of all shapes and sizes, some more humanoid than others.

Kyle and I weren't unfamiliar with swinger parties and other events in the LGBTQ community, and we had gone to a few of them in our younger years. After we got legally married, we settled into comfortable monogamy. But seeing the monsters show up in our world had been interesting to both of us. It felt a bit like a fantasy movie come to life. And many of the monsters seemed just as fascinated by humans as we were with them. One evening, I made a comment that I don't even fully remember about how I wondered if the monsters could have sex with humans. Kyle had looked at me much more seriously than I had figured he would and said, "Would you want to have sex with a monster?"

The question had surprised me and also had made me

think. I had never considered myself one of those "monster fucker" type people who read monster romance novels or watched movies and thought about banging the creature. I had always been happy and content with Kyle. But, I realized, the idea was a little intriguing. "Maybe," I had said. "Would you?"

Kyle nodded. "I think it could be fun and interesting."

I knew he didn't mean it as any sort of slight against me; we had always been very open and honest with one another about our likes, dislikes, and the frequency of our sex life. But now I was strangely curious too. "I'd be game if you are," I said, surprising myself more than a little. "But only if it's both of us together."

"Oh, a monster threesome?" Kyle asked in a sing-song tone that made me blush. I was a little more private about my sexuality than many others in our community. Plus, a threesome sounded like something for our 20's, not for our late 40's or early 50's. But Kyle laughed and squeezed my hand. "Why don't I do some digging and see what I can find, all right? You can always change your mind."

Kyle looked into it, and one of his students, who knew far too much about monsters than any middle schooler should, told him about the Monster Match dating app out there. Curious as always, Kyle dug further and found one of the monsters on the app owned a deep-sea fishing excursion boat for rent. And, as if the universe had decided to give us a special gift for my birthday, this blue creature with a long snout and kind-looking eyes had listed that he was interested in having a good time without a committed relationship. "Should we ask him if he'd be interested in a threesome?" Kyle said as he showed me the pictures on the app of the strange, blue creature that I had never seen before.

I had never been confident in approaching people for things like sexual encounters; Kyle was much more outgoing than I was. This sea creature was certainly interesting, the bright blue of his skin different than anything I had seen before. I supposed if we were going to go all-in on fucking a monster, why not go with one who didn't look remotely human? "You ask him," I said, giving Kyle my patented shy-guy smile.

"I will!" Kyle declared.

And he had. He had told me about Glauruss and the plan to rent his boat and go fishing for my birthday, and the threesome that the monster had agreed to. And then, he died. The swim trunks we had ordered still sat in their plastic wrap in the delivery box, our new sandals on top of them. The last plans we had made together for the future. The future that we had not been able to have.

I clicked on the 'Respond to message' button in the email notification, not really sure what else to do. Kyle hadn't put any money down for the trip yet, as far as I knew. But we had definitely ghosted the monster we had asked to have a threesome with, and that didn't sit right with me. Even if we hadn't met him in person, I still thought it would at least be polite to let him know what happened.

The app opened up to the chat, and I could see the messages between Kyle and Glauruss, going back and forth, discussing what we were looking for and making plans for my birthday that was still a few weeks away. Kyle had sounded so excited about it all, and that brought a little smile to my lips. I began to type.

FabTeacher: Hi Glauruss. This is Reuben, Kyle's husband. I'm sorry to tell you this but Kyle died. I just logged into his email to find this account.

I went back to looking through Kyle's email, but after only a few minutes, a chat notification popped up, and I opened the Monster Match app to see what it said.

SeaKing Swimmer: omg, I'm so sorry! What happened?

For some reason, I hadn't really been expecting to hear back from the sea dragon, and especially not so quickly. But here he was, online, wanting information. I opened the app again.

FabTeacher: An accident.

He began to type back almost instantly, so I sat and stared at the screen until four little words popped up.

SeaKing Swimmer: How are you doing?

Four little words from someone I had never talked to before, words that could be flippantly tossed around but, right now, meant the world to me for reasons I didn't understand. My social human brain wanted to type back *Good*, or *As well as can be expected*, or something equally reassuring to not make him feel uncomfortable. But I couldn't. I had been putting on a brave face as well as I could, but I was exhausted and overwhelmed and lost. And I didn't have to speak to Glauruss again if I didn't want to. So, I responded honestly.

FabTeacher: Not well. It's been really rough and I'm so tired.

I wondered if my words would turn him off, and he would just come back with some sort of apology and then an excuse to not speak to me again. But the little dots formed, and, a moment later, his response came through.

SeaKing Swimmer: I know how that feels. I'm sure you have a lot going on but if youd like to talk to someone we could get together.

That stopped my mind-spiral in its tracks. That wasn't

just a generic nicety. I was feeling alone and abandoned in many ways, and maybe this monster knew how that felt. And, as strange as it was, going to the beach to meet Glauruss like Kyle had planned for us to do actually sounded kind of nice. So, I typed out a message back.

FabTeacher: I think I'd like that. When?
SeaKing Swimmer: I'm free this Sunday.
FabTeacher: That works. When and where?
SeaKing Swimmer: 1pm? There's a stand on the boardwalk called Bayside Breeze.
FabTeacher: Sounds good, I'll see you then
SeaKing Swimmer: Great!

Had I really just done that? Set up a meeting with a monster to commiserate about my dead husband? A monster that he and I had been planning to have sex with? For some reason, that thought made my ears burn. But what really got under my skin was me realizing that that would be what Kyle would want. He loved meeting new people and being social; while I was more of a homebody, he was always interested in making new friends and having new experiences. I thought he would be proud of me taking the steps to meet someone on my own, and a monster, no less.

And then my mind turned back to the task at hand. I had to reach out to so many places and let them know Kyle was dead. Some of our joint accounts probably wouldn't matter as much, would they? I didn't even know. And how was I supposed to figure it out? There was so much paper. A lifetime spread out before me as numbers and dates and dollar signs. Things as simple as a receipt for the lunch we had out a few days before Kyle died. The warranty for our new water heater after our old one stopped working. Paystubs, tax forms, flyers, computer printouts, bank statements, correspondence from former students, and receipts, so many fucking receipts. There was enough paper that I thought I could be crushed under its weight. Buried alive in a coffin of grocery store coupons and mortgage statements.

I didn't even know where to start. My job was numbers and paperwork, yet I sat in front of the computer like I had never seen one before. I clicked the mouse to open an internet browser. The address bar cursor blinked at me, waiting for me to tell it where to go. Where was I supposed to go? What did I need to do?

My lungs suddenly felt like they had shrunk inside of me. My next breath was a struggle. Sweat broke out across my skin, almost instantly soaking my shirt at the neck and back. I felt the *thump-thump* of my heart in my chest, getting stronger and stronger like it was trying to break its way free from my ribcage. A heart attack! I was having a fucking heart attack!

For one tense moment, I debated just letting it take me. Let someone find me in the house, surrounded by memories of Kyle, alone and lost. If I just let go, I'd die, and then this pain would be over. The loss, the sorrow, the desperate longing. If there was an afterlife, maybe I'd even see Kyle again. Even just seeing him long enough to tell him I loved him one more time would be enough.

Heat blossomed in my face, and I realized with startling clarity that I didn't want to die. Kyle wouldn't want that for me. He would want me to live and take care of myself, since he wasn't there to do it. And, as much as I hated to admit it, I was scared. Death was final, and there was so much to live for. I wanted to finish the new season of the fantasy TV show that Kyle and I had been watching together so I could know how it ended and tell him. I wanted to eat Chinese food again, even without him there to tease me for my spice aversion. I wanted to go deep-sea fishing like we had been planning for my birthday. I wanted to meet Glauruss on Sunday. I couldn't do any of those things if I was dead.

My hand shook so badly, I wasn't sure if I'd be able to even dial my phone. I swiped up, but my eyes were blurry as I stared at the number keys for my passcode that suddenly seemed hopelessly too small for me. I knew there were a few ways to activate an emergency call on my phone, but damned if I could think of any of them right now as my brain seemed to freeze inside my head. Sweat poured down my face and dripped onto my phone screen. I was going to die because I couldn't remember how to call for help on my stupid phone.

Somehow, I think I was able to hit the emergency button,

because I heard a very faint voice come from my phone that sounded authoritative. My mouth had suddenly gone extremely dry, despite the fact that I was soaked in sweat, my eyes stinging from the fat droplets running down my forehead into them. "H... help... Heart attack," I said, hoping that the person on the other end of the line could hear me, because I could not figure out how to put the phone on speaker. I heard a tinny response, but I couldn't make out the words. I think I mumbled my address as I clutched my chest, struggling to breathe, to make my eyes focus, to make my limbs cooperate with me. Time seemed to slow to a crawl, each agonizing second made longer by the inability to breathe or control my own body.

I heard sirens approaching, so far away that it sounded like I was under water. I tried to get out of my chair to open the door, but my body still was not listening to me, and I found myself stuck in my chair like a sea turtle wedged in a crevice. The front door was locked, but thankfully, I had left the front window open to catch the breeze, so the smaller of the two paramedics pushed out the screen and climbed inside. He let his partner in, and then both of them were at my side, checking my vitals, putting an oxygen mask over my face, lifting me onto a gurney as they asked questions that I could not process for the life of me.

They took me to Gilmer Hospital in an ambulance. A lot of that day was a blur. I remember being in the hospital room. I was aware that they took blood for tests, and I had an IV attached to my hand. I was put into multiple scanning machines with various electrodes hooked up to my body. Machines beeped at every imaginable pitch and speed until I was hearing phantom beeps even when there were none. I was given a meal at some point, though what it was or how much I ate, I still can't remember. I also wondered if I was hallucinating at one point, because I saw what looked like a purple demon with curving horns walk down the hallway past my room before remembering that monsters were a thing. The purple creature gave me a beaming smile, much brighter than I had received from anyone recently. It made me feel warmer and more relaxed as I waited in the white room with the beeping machines.

Finally, Dr. Ross came to talk to me. I had not had a heart attack, as I had initially thought, she informed me. I had had a panic attack, which could be mistaken for a heart attack because of the similar symptoms and stressful situations. I had never had a panic attack before.

"Are you under a lot of stress right now?" Dr. Ross asked. "Any major life changes?"

The questions were so absurd, I nearly laughed. Only the tightness in my chest kept me from a rude-sounding guffaw. "My... my husband just died," I said, pressing a hand to my chest as it twinged with the effort of breathing.

"Ah. Yes, that would do it," Dr. Ross said, giving me that small, sympathetic smile I had grown so used to recently. "It's a lot to process all at once." Oh, how right she was about that. "Is this the first panic attack you've had since your husband died?"

I nodded slowly. Was this going to happen again? I really didn't need the added stress of anticipating a random feeling like I was suffocating on top of everything else right now.

"I don't think we would want to put you on medication unless panic attacks become a regular occurrence," Dr. Ross told me. "We can recommend therapy, especially grief counseling."

I didn't know how effective grief counseling might actually be. If it wasn't one on one, I wasn't necessarily interested either. The idea of being in a group with a bunch of people who had also faced a traumatic loss sounded both depressing and nerve-wracking to me. But, either way, I had to get out of the hospital and take care of myself. I couldn't do anything from my hospital bed except feel bad, and I had had enough of that to last me a lifetime.

I was released later that evening. I took a car home, glad to see that no one had broken into my house while I had been at the hospital. I had to find a video online to figure out how to fix the screen the paramedic had pushed out on the window. I had never been the handiest person, but I thought Kyle would be proud of me.

Thursday, the day after my panic attack, I gave myself

permission to do nothing. I only did things that I felt I was able to. I ordered in food, I looked through the cards from the funeral again, I watched TV. I knew I had things I needed to do, but they could wait a day for me to feel like myself again.

"How do you eat an elephant?" Kyle used to ask. "One bite at a time."

Teaching middle school English, Kyle had been a fountain of dad jokes, silly words of wisdom, and educational anecdotes. That was what I needed right now. I had a whole elephant to eat, and I would just have to take it one bite at a time. One phone call, one email, one mailed envelope, until it was done. So, Friday and Saturday, I sat down at the computer with my phone and started the tedious process of closing down Kyle's affairs.

Despite our tech-savvy world, we lived in a country and a time when handling someone's affairs after death was surprisingly difficult. Maybe it was just that no one really liked to think about death, but it was much harder to close out someone's life than it seemed like it should have been. I repeated, "My name is Reuben Thompson. My husband, Kyle Thompson, had an account with you. He recently passed away," so many times that it became almost automatic when I spoke to someone new on the phone. And then there would be the awkward pause as the person on the other end processed this information and then usually responded with an attempted sympathetic, "Oh, I'm so sorry to hear that.

Um, hold on, let me find out how to handle this."

Some of it was easy enough to manage; our shared bank accounts were also in my name, so I was able to transfer some payments and bills over to my account instead. I cancelled several of his subscriptions to various magazines and educational courses. It felt so strange to do that. Kyle had spent his life teaching children and serving others, and now that life was suddenly gone. Everything that he had been doing or that he had been involved in continued on without him. It was a strange dichotomy. The world kept moving, plunging heartlessly ahead, not stopping to let me get my bearings or catch my breath, like waves crashing onto a beach. But, at the same time, my own little world had stopped. I was drifting on the waves, lost at sea, with nothing to anchor me in place and no idea how to signal for help or communicate my distress.

I answered my phone every time it rang, since I was not sure what might be relevant to Kyle or not. That meant I got a lot of spam calls, which only added to my mental exhaustion. I wished there was a 'going through some shit, do not call me right now' option. When I heard the telltale click of a machine picking up or the familiar recorded messages about car warranties, loans, and other junk calls, I hung up as quickly as I could. I was half worried that if I actually spoke to a person, I might break down and start screaming, and that was not something I wanted to do. Those two days passed in a sort of fog. I ate, I slept, I somehow kept myself alive without being entirely aware of it. It was a relief when Sunday finally came.

Chapter 5

Glauruss

I was surprisingly nervous about meeting with Reuben. I don't know why. Maybe it was just the whole "we were all planning to have sex together" thing. Or the awkwardness of knowing that his husband had passed away and my only connection to him had been online.

I strolled up the beach on Sunday, the sand clinging to my damp feet as I walked. The ground was burning hot, but I barely felt it. My sleek skin was designed to withstand both extreme temperatures and extreme pressure, as I could dive deeper into the ocean than any human could. The sun beating down on me did dry up my skin fairly quickly when I was out of the water, but as long as I stayed hydrated and went back in the water by the end of the day, I would be just fine.

My appearance drew glances from everyone on the beach. More than one group of humans stopped and stared. I didn't blame them. While monsters were becoming more and more common in the area, a good lot of them were relatively humanoid. I, with my bright blue skin, elongated snout, long tail, and various fins coming off of me, only vaguely resembled anything close to human. I was not much taller or broader than most humans though, which was surprisingly helpful. If I had had to navigate the human world while being monstrously taller or bigger than the average human, I'm sure it would have been much more difficult for me. Luckily, the human world was over 70% water, if I remembered correctly, and I was able to survive and breathe in both fresh and salt water, my unique skin filtering out any unusable minerals from my body. So, I was at least able to navigate the human world with relative ease, though I loved its giant oceans best of all, as they reminded me of my home in the monster world.

I made my way up the beach to the boardwalk, where brightly-colored squat buildings sat. Various restaurants, treat takeaway counters, and overpriced souvenir stands lined the beach, and hawkers walked amongst the beachgoers with sunglasses, light-up toys, and other trinkets for kids. I had told Reuben to meet me at Bayside Breeze, a little tropical-inspired hut where my friend worked and had some of the best cocktails on the boardwalk.

I recognized Reuben right away from pictures Kyle had

sent me. He was a big man, though it was hard to tell how tall he was, as he was sitting on a stool at the bar. He had on a faded, black tee-shirt, a pair of blue swim trunks, and sandals on his bare feet. His black, curly hair was cropped short on his head, and he had a moustache and beard that were also short. He had gray around his temples and in several other places. I knew humans often got gray or white hair when they got older or when they were stressed. I was sure that he was definitely the latter. He had on a pair of sunglasses, but he pushed them up onto his head as he saw me approaching. He had a kind, soft face, but his brown eyes looked tired, dark bags under them. I gave him a smile, careful to keep my mouth closed. My sharp teeth could sometimes be intimidating when I first met people. I lifted my hand to wave, and he waved back. His sunglasses slid back down his face and bopped him on the nose. He grabbed them and pulled them off with a sheepish look, setting them on the bar next to his glass of ice water instead.

I stopped a few feet from him. "Reuben?" He nodded, and I smiled again. "Hi. I'm Glauruss."

"Pleased to meet you," Reuben said. He held out his hand to me to shake.

That was rather unusual. Most people were rather startled by my appearance. I gingerly placed my palm into his own, curling my wispy fingers around his as best I could, giving his hand a polite shake in return. He looked rather surprised at the touch.

"Sorry," I said, pulling my hand back and wiggling my fingers a bit. My palm was as solid as his, but my fingers were more like small tentacles; I could move them every which direction independently, even bending them completely backwards or scrunching them down into almost nothing. It was all very helpful when swimming or hunting fish. "That probably felt weird."

He gave a slightly awkward chuckle. "That's okay. I wasn't really sure what to expect anyway." He gestured to the empty stool next to him. "Um, wanna sit down? Have a drink?" I nodded and slid onto the stool, letting my tail relax and hang down behind me. He did not have a drink in front of him besides his water. "What would you like?"

"Whatever you're going to have is fine," I said. "I am not particular, as long as it's alcohol."

Reuben looked like he might laugh, but instead, just the corners of his mouth quirked up in a smile. "Even if it's some super sweet, fruity thing?"

"I love super sweet and fruity! As long as it has at least one cherry," I said with a grin. I was strangely partial to sweet things. It's not like the raw fish I usually ate for food were all that sweet, or even very flavorful. Maraschino cherries had become my fruit of choice when it came to cocktails.

Reuben turned back to the bartender. His name was Mike, and he knew me very well from my couple years working on the oceanfront. So, when Reuben requested a fruit punch cocktail with cherries, I knew Mike would add a few extra to my glass. We sat for a moment as Mike turned to start working on our drinks. Reuben gave me a slightly self-conscious smile, but he didn't say anything.

Was it better to just rip the bandage off? Or was it better to dance awkwardly around each other? I was not much for dancing. "I'm sure you're tired of hearing it, but I'm so sorry about Kyle," I said, tipping my head sympathetically toward him.

Reuben's small smile didn't change, but his face suddenly looked much sadder than it had a moment ago. "Thank you," he said softly. And then he went silent again.

When he didn't say anything else, I decided to keep talking. "I'm sorry I didn't get to meet him in person," I said.

"You would have liked him, I think," Reuben said, drawing the tip of his finger through a ring of condensation from his water on the bar top. "He was everybody's friend."

"Do you want to talk about him?" I asked.

Reuben looked up at me, genuine surprise on his face. I stared back at him, afraid I had said the wrong thing. But he surprised me by saying, "No one has asked me that."

I stared at him, tipping my head curiously again. "Really?"

"Really," Reuben said. His right hand moved to toy with the gold band on his left hand. A wedding band, I knew, from the number of weddings I had been part of on my boat. "I think there's this fear of bringing it up. Like it will be too painful to talk about."

"I'm sure it is painful," I agreed, giving him another soft

smile. "But that doesn't mean we need to hide from it."

Reuben lifted his eyes to meet mine. They were a warm brown, with little crinkles at the corners of his eyes that only deepened when he smiled. I liked them. "I... I'd like to talk about him with you. But isn't it weird to talk about past relationships with someone you're just meeting?"

I shrugged. "I don't find it weird. But we can talk about whatever you want." If he was not feeling comfortable talking about Kyle with me, I was not about to pressure him into it.

Reuben smiled, and then it grew even brighter as Mike set down two cheery red drinks in front of us, with a whole ton of fruit on skewers in it, including extra cherries for me. He picked up his glass, holding it out to me. "Cheers to... being alive."

I picked up my own glass and clinked it against his. "Being alive," I agreed before taking a large sip.

Reuben took his own sip. "Oh wow, that's pretty good!"

"Mike makes good cocktails," I said, giving the bartender a nod and a smile that showed my sharp teeth. He chuckled and nodded back to me as he set about mixing other drinks. "So, what would you like to talk about?"

Reuben flushed a little. "I... I'm not great at small talk. What do you want to talk about?"

"I wanna know about you," I said, crunching a chunk of pineapple, outside and all, between my teeth. The sour sweetness was delightful. "What do you do? For a living, I mean."

"Oh," Reuben said, seeming fascinated by me eating the spiny outside of the pineapple with no problem. "Nothing really interesting. I'm a financial analyst at a bank."

"So, you like numbers?" I asked curiously. I had no idea what a 'financial analyst' did, but I knew banks were about numbers and money.

Reuben chuckled softly. "I guess you could say that. I went to school for business. I've always liked math. Numbers don't lie."

"Never been much good with numbers myself," I said, smiling without teeth again. "But I only really learned them when I came here to the human world."

Reuben nodded thoughtfully. "I doubt there's much need for numbers in the monster world. What brought you here anyway? To the human world, I mean."

I shrugged a little. "Sheer curiosity."

"Really, that's it? Just curiosity?" Reuben asked, taking a large swallow of his drink.

I shrugged again. "I didn't have anything that I was living for in the other world. I thought, why not try something new? I wasn't going to be missed anyway."

Reuben frowned. "That can't be true. Didn't you have friends? Family?"

"We are not the most social of species in the monster world," I said thoughtfully. "We form small family units. But mine..." I paused and gazed back at him. I had never shared my story with anyone before, and I wasn't entirely sure I wanted to dump it all on Reuben so early on. Especially when I knew he was dealing with so much. "It's a story best left for later." I knocked back the rest of my drink, including the ice, in one gulp. I motioned at Mike, and he nodded.

Reuben blinked in surprise for a moment, but then he nodded and took another long drink of his punch. "Got it. Um, how about your work here? You take people out on boats?"

At least my job was something I could talk about a little easier. "Yes. I take people out on my boat for various things. Weddings, fishing expeditions, scientific work, whatever people want to do on the open ocean."

"That sounds pretty neat," Reuben said. "Do you like it?"

I chuckled as Mike set down a tall whiskey sour next to me, with a skewer of cherries. "Yeah, it's pretty fun. I have to be near the water anyway, so why not make money from it, you know?"

Reuben nodded. "Makes sense. But obviously you can…" He gestured vaguely to me with one large hand. "Be out of water too?"

I grinned with teeth this time, and I saw him tense for just a moment. I quickly closed my lips around my sharp teeth again. "Yes. For about a day. And I can go in both fresh and salt water, so as long as I have a body of water nearby, I'm pretty good."

Reuben crunched his pineapple between his teeth. He did

not eat the spiny outside the way I did. "Is the water here different from the monster world?"

"A little," I said. "Different acidity, different creatures in it."

"I'd love to see your boat sometime," Reuben said. "It sounds pretty neat."

I sat up a bit straighter, even my tail perking up from where it drooped. "You would?"

He nodded. "To be honest, I've never been much of a water person. Or, I guess, I should say, I haven't had many opportunities to go out on the water."

"Really? Even living this close to the ocean?" I asked curiously.

Reuben looked sheepish again. "Yeah. I don't know why, really."

"Well, let's change that," I said, knocking the rest of my drink back with one swallow that burned all the way down. "Come on, I'll show it to you right now."

Reuben nodded, reaching into his pocket for his wallet, but I waved my hand. "I got it. Mike, put it on my tab."

"Sure thing, Blue," Mike said.

"Are you sure? I don't mind paying," Reuben offered.

I shook my head. "My treat, seriously."

"Okay." His smile was soft but so sweet. "So, you know the bartender?" he asked as we started to walk along the beach toward the docks.

"Yeah. His name's Mike," I said. "He owns that little

stand. Good guy, was one of my first friends when I started working in this area."

"He seems like a nice guy."

"He is," I agreed.

"So, what made you specifically decide to take people out on a boat as a job?" Reuben asked.

"It wasn't my first job when I arrived here in the human world," I said thoughtfully, side-stepping two kids who had stopped playing with a beach ball right in my path to stare. I gave them a friendly smile, and they still just stared. At least they didn't scream or cry, which was not an unusual reaction, especially from younger children. "I first worked for a construction company; they had some underwater projects that I was able to help with, since I can dive deeper than humans can."

Reuben was gazing at me with rapt attention. I wondered if he had ever met a monster before, or if he was just very interested in what I had to say. "But I left them, decided to start my own business."

"You said you take people out for like weddings and stuff?"

I nodded. "Or whatever people want to do on a boat. I've had like birthdays, bachelorette parties, stuff like that. I took out some guys who were studying dolphins or something. It's been interesting, seeing different kinds of humans."

Reuben rubbed thoughtfully at his short beard with his hand. "What about the Monster Match app?"

"What about it?" I asked, and his cheeks flushed a deep red beneath his dark skin.

"What are you looking for on there?"

"Oh," I said, giving him a smile that I hoped would put him at ease. "Anything, really. It's good for networking, and people like the novelty of monsters, which is good for business."

"So, you're not like actually looking for a relationship?" Reuben asked.

"Why? Are you offering?" I teased.

Reuben's face went scarlet, and I could have kicked myself. The guy had just lost his husband, and here I was making sex jokes. "Sorry. Bad joke. I can be a bit of a flirt," I confessed.

Reuben smiled, his big hands twitching a little by his sides like he was uncomfortable. "It's all right. Sorry, I'm just... curious. And nervous. Really nervous."

"Why?" I asked in surprise.

"I don't know," Reuben admitted with a small shrug.

"Well, just to be clear, I'm not planning to jump your bones or anything," I offered, trying to lighten him up.

He laughed. It was a nice sound, very deep and carefree. "I appreciate that. I'm not much in the mood for... that... right now."

"I understand," I said, dipping my head a bit. "It's different without your husband here."

He nodded, his eyes turning to look out at the blue

ocean. "I thought that he and I would be coming out here together."

We arrived at the pier where there were multiple boats docked, of various sizes and uses. My boat did not stand out very differently from the other boats anchored there. I stepped onto the dock and started toward my boat. I glanced back. Reuben was stepping cautiously onto the dock like he expected the whole thing to rock like a rope bridge. I tried not to laugh and offered him a hand. "Here. 'Til you get your sea legs."

He took my hand with another sheepish smile. "Sorry. I'm just really not used to water."

"It's all right," I said, trying to soothe him without sounding condescending. "I won't let you fall in."

He laughed nervously, watching the wood beneath his sandals, and his hand tightened in mine. We walked down the dock until we reached my boat. "Here we are, home sweet home."

Reuben looked up, and I noticed his eye immediately go to the name painted on the side in blue letters. 'Dragon U2C Stuff.' He let out another of those deep laughs. "Wow, that's... that's clever."

I grinned. "Thanks, I thought so. Wait here." I let go of his hand, hopping the distance onto the boat. He looked worried for a second until I extended the gangplank for him to board, offering him my hand again. He walked carefully over the gangplank and the few steps onto the boat, and I could feel him shaking a little bit. "You all right?" I asked as he made it onto the deck.

He let out a puff of air. "Yeah. Just, the water moving takes some getting used to."

I motioned to the center of the boat where there was a covered dining-room type space. "Here, wanna sit until you're used to the water?"

He nodded gratefully, and I led him inside, steering him into one of the chairs in the space. I headed to the bar. "Can I get you something to drink?"

"Just water would be great," he said. I grabbed a bottle of cold water for him and filled a glass with ice for myself before grabbing a bottle of birthday cake-flavored vodka and taking it all back to him. I sat down in one of the other chairs as he toyed with the label on the plastic bottle. He looked extremely awkward. He had said he wasn't good at small talk, and I was learning that pretty quickly. "Would you like to tell me about Kyle?" I asked. "How did you two meet?"

He immediately softened at my words. I wondered if he had gone through the past week feeling like he couldn't say anything, for fear of upsetting himself or someone else. "We met in college. He was in the year below me, studying education, and I studied business. But we actually met at the college's gay-straight alliance club."

"That must have been a long time ago," I said.

Reuben nodded. "Feels like a lifetime ago. I had more hair then too."

"Oh yeah?" I asked, tipping my head curiously.

"Yeah, like a full..." He waved his hands a little, trying to demonstrate. "Wait, I have a picture."

He pulled out his phone and started scrolling on it. I swallowed a mouthful of sweet vodka and poured another, taking two swallows before he held up his phone for me to see.

Young Reuben stood in a long, black gown. His hair was much puffier then, standing out on both sides of his head from under a flat, four-cornered hat, looking almost like pom-poms on either side of his head. He did not have his moustache and beard either, giving him a baby-faced appearance. He held a black leather cover and was giving the camera a big, toothy grin. Next to him stood a man and a woman that I assumed were his parents, the woman in a blue dress as she clung to Reuben's arm with a smile just as big and bright. He got his body shape from his father, but I could see his mother all over his smile and the crinkle of his eyes. "This was when I graduated college," he said with a chuckle. "First one in my family to go. My momma was so proud."

"You *did* have hair then," I said, waving at one of the puffs with a fluttery fingertip.

"Yeah," he laughed. "I started cutting it short a few years later. Looked more 'professional.'" He said this with a hint of bitterness that I hadn't heard from him before. That made me wonder; I saw people with all kinds of hair on the beach.

I had not a single hair on my own body.

"Isn't your own natural hair professional?"

Reuben shook his head. "Surprisingly, no. Humans have very strange ideas about what's okay and what's not."

"Huh." I mused on this as I swallowed the rest of the vodka in my glass. Why would a natural part of your body not be considered professional? It wasn't like his hair would get in his way doing bank stuff. "Do you still have parents?"

He blinked, and I realized my question was both oddly-phrased and also probably rude. But he just gave me a small smile. "My momma passed away about eight years ago from breast cancer. My dad is still alive, but he's in a care facility about two hours from here. He's got advanced dementia."

"What is that?"

"Oh. It's a... memory loss mental thing," he tried to explain. "He doesn't usually recognize people or know where he is or what's going on."

I frowned a bit. "That sounds rough."

He nodded. "Yeah. My younger sister, Brenda, is the only other family that I have left on my side. She has three kids, my nephews and niece."

He did not mention Kyle's family, and I assumed that they were probably not in the picture either. I had learned early on during my time in the human world that 'being gay' was still not fully accepted by everyone, which seemed ridiculous to me, especially for such an advanced species. Love was love, and family was family.

Reuben held up his phone. There was a picture of two men standing side by side, both wearing white suits with blue bowties and shiny, black shoes. I recognized one of them to be a younger version of Reuben, still with a round, smiling face, but hardly any gray in his hair, and he had a beard now. Next to him stood a white man with brown hair, a hawk-like nose and kind, brown eyes. Their arms were around one another, and there was a two-layer cake behind them, decorated with white icing and blue roses. "This was our wedding."

My species does not get 'married' in the way that humans did, but I had seen several weddings take place on boats and on the beach. I knew it was a happy occasion, with family and friends and lots of music, dancing, and drinking. Reuben and Kyle looked so happy, standing together, gold wedding bands on their fingers. "It's beautiful," I commented. "This doesn't look like that long ago."

Reuben nodded. "We got married when it became legal here. But we had been together for over 20 years before that."

That made me a little sad, to think that Reuben and Kyle had been together in a committed relationship for so long but unable to make it legal. The human world was so strange sometimes, with all of its 'legalities' and 'laws' that dictated what people could and could not do.

"What about you?" Reuben asked, putting his phone back into his pocket and taking a sip from his water.

"What about me, what?" I asked, blinking. I was feeling very warm and heavy from all the alcohol I had drunk.

"Did you have a... significant other in the monster world? Parents? Kids?"

The words hit me like a blow to the chest. I cleared my throat hard, the sound raspy. "I, uh..." My throat suddenly felt too tight, and I swallowed the rest of my drink, ice cubes and all, the icy points digging into my esophagus as they traveled down my body. I knew this question had been coming, but now that it had, I suddenly had no idea what to say.

Reuben gazed at me for a long moment before I think he realized my discomfort. "Oh, I'm sorry," he said softly. "We don't... I didn't mean..."

I shook my head, much too hard and much too fast. "No, it's fine. You're fine. I just..." I held up my hands like I was holding words in them I couldn't say.

"We don't have to talk about it," Reuben said gently. "I... honestly should go anyway. Tomorrow is my first day back to work after... everything."

I nodded, lurching to my feet and offering my hand. "Yeah, no problem. It was nice to meet you."

"Nice to meet you too," he said, taking my hand and giving it a polite shake.

It was only after he was halfway down the dock that I realized I should have helped him on the gangplank and offered to escort him back to the beach. But it was silly to go chasing after him now, and, with my current state, I might possibly end up in the water. All right for me, of course, but not all right for him. I poured myself another drink.

Chapter 6

Reuben

I finally had to go back to work on Monday. I put on my usual suit and tie; I had always preferred t-shirts and shorts, but in the corporate world, a suit was your armor and your shield. Anything less, and you might as well be in your underwear. Walking into the office that first morning back, I wasn't sure what to expect. My manager had at least been understanding of the situation, which I knew was a blessing that many people did not have when it came to emergencies. It was a strange mixture of people being exceptionally quiet and awkward around me, and others being overly friendly and helpful. But oddly enough, no one mentioned Kyle by name. In fact, very few of them even asked me how I was feeling. It seemed like an unspoken rule that they did not want to mention any unpleasantness that could result in making me upset, so everyone just sort of danced around it.

And then there was my meeting yesterday with Glauruss that kept replaying in my head. I hesitated to call what we had a date, since we hadn't really agreed that it was a date, just getting together to talk. He had been nice. He seemed to genuinely care how I felt about what was going on. But I noticed how quickly he knocked back all of his drinks at the Bayside Breeze. I had thought that by us going to his boat, he might be done drinking, but I had been wrong. And the fact that every time I had mentioned family, he had clammed up and gotten really uncomfortable. There was something painful there, something that he did not want to talk about. Which I could understand. Perhaps it was something I could help with, but he and I barely knew each other. We had not yet established that relationship, that bond of trust and friendship.

I actually wondered if I would hear from him again at all. We had not left on the best terms. If I didn't hear from him by Wednesday, I figured I'd write back and at least apologize for anything I said that caused him pain. But I actually got a notification in Kyle's email Tuesday night that there was a message from Glauruss. I opened it up.

SeaKing Swimmer: Hey sorry about Sunday. You didn't do anything wrong I just have a hard time talking about family. Do you want to get together again?

That question made me think. We could easily go our separate ways now if we wanted. But having someone who hadn't known Kyle and didn't find it as awkward when I talked about him was kind of nice. And it got me out of the house. I didn't want to turn into a complete hermit with Kyle gone. That wasn't healthy for me. So, I wrote back.

FabTeacher: That's ok, we both have stuff we're dealing with. I'd like to get together again. When?

SeaKing Swimmer: Sunday same time again?

FabTeacher: Works for me!

SeaKing Swimmer: I'll meet you at the dock, we can hang out on my boat? Maybe take it out for a bit?

FabTeacher: Sounds good, as long as I don't fall over board!

SeaKing Swimmer: I promise I wont let you!!

I had until Sunday before I saw Glauruss again. This was going to be a long week.

And it was. I found myself vacillating between depression and anger. More than once, I had a breakdown in my office at work and had to lock myself in a bathroom stall until the tears passed, my fist pressed against my mouth to muffle the screams that tried to break free. It would come out of nowhere, which was more than a little frustrating. But I supposed grief wasn't on a schedule.

My fifty-first birthday came and went, like any other day. No one remembered. I barely even remembered myself, which was all right with me. I spent the evening on the couch with a half-gallon of cookie dough ice cream and finished the television series Kyle and I had been watching. When I went to bed that night, I cried and held Kyle's urn in my arms.

I decided on Saturday to drive the two hours one way to go visit my dad. It had been about six weeks since I had visited him; Kyle and I had planned to go see him again soon. I wanted to tell him about Kyle, though I had no idea if he would actually remember him, or even me.

One of the nurses at the care center escorted me to his room. I had brought a box of chocolate raspberry cremes, his favorite candy, and I set it on the little table nearby. "Hi, Dad," I said as I sat down in the chair next to the bed.

Benjamin Thompson gazed back at me, the whites of his eyes more of an ivory now. He had been a large man in his youth; his whole side of the family had always been 'big boned.' But his ailing mental health had obviously taken its toll on his body, his skin loose and wrinkled. He had been such a strong man up until my momma passed away. I wondered if I was looking at my future self. Would my mind start to go too as I got older, living alone without my spouse by my side?

"Hello," he rasped politely, but there was no recognition of me in his face.

I took his hand in mine. He had big hands, but the skin was stretched taut over the bones. He was definitely frailer than he had been the last time I came to see him. I had a sinking feeling in my gut that he was not much longer for this world.

"I wanted to let you know, Kyle passed away recently," I said, keeping my voice gentle so as not to disturb him. My father looked at me, and I could see that the name held no meaning for him. "My husband, Kyle," I added. Still nothing.

"I'm sorry, Jacob," my father said, patting my thigh with his withered hand. "I'm sure you'll see him again soon."

Jacob was my father's younger brother, the uncle that had died more than thirty years ago from a drug overdose. But the fact that my dad associated any name with me at all in his advanced dementia was a blessing.

"Yeah, I probably will."

"When is Linda coming to visit?" he asked me.

My momma, Linda, had been dead for eight years now. When my father's memory had started to go and he would ask that question, myself or one of the nurses would gently remind him that Linda was dead. But every time I said it, I saw the hope die in the old man's eyes, the desolation and sorrow that passed over him. Kyle had been the first one to answer, "She's coming tomorrow, Benny." That simple statement had made my dad's eyes light up like a Christmas tree. I worried that the lie would hurt him, that he would be devastated the next day when his wife never appeared. But my father had not seemed to remember, asking us again when Linda was coming. 'Tomorrow' was always the answer, even though 'tomorrow' never came. I knew one of these days, it would; he would leave this life and be reunited with my momma. "She's coming tomorrow, Dad."

He seemed satisfied with that answer, his lips curling back in a sort of grotesque way. He squeezed my hand. "What's your name?"

"Reuben," I said.

"Reu... ben..." He said the word like it meant something to him, and hope sparked in my chest. But then he turned eyes back to the ceiling and went quiet, and the hope faded again.

I couldn't help but wonder if I would suffer the same fate when I got older, having my brain turn on me, making me afraid of people around me or unable to comprehend who or what was happening or where I was. If I had had Kyle by my side for it, I imagined it would be better. I could only hope that if it did ever come to that, someone would be kind enough to tell me 'tomorrow' when I looked for Kyle.

I held my father's hand until he fell asleep, and then I still just sat there, keeping ahold of him. Another long goodbye. It had been the same way with my momma, with months of deteriorating health as the cancer ravaged her body. It had been almost a relief when she had passed. I thought that it might be the same when the time came for my dad. Was a long goodbye better than no goodbye at all? Why did it seem like there was no medium between suddenly gone and hanging on but not really there? I wondered if perhaps Kyle and I would have had a long goodbye, one of us getting sick as we grew older together. Would that have been easier to handle? It was silly to speculate, but there was that little part of me that I knew would always wonder *'what if?'*

Chapter 7

Glauruss

When Reuben arrived on Sunday, I was waiting for him at the end of the dock to walk him carefully down to my boat and help him aboard. His smile was so kind and sunny, even though his eyes still spoke of exhaustion and sadness.

I admit I was several drinks in by the time Reuben arrived, though I wasn't sure how obvious it was. I had learned that there was such a thing as a 'functioning alcoholic,' which described me accurately at that time. I could hold things together relatively well, I figured. The one thing I would not do was take my boat out when I had been drinking though, and I made the excuse to Reuben that the water was too choppy today, which was sort of true with the high winds.

We sat in the lounge area again. He only asked for water when I offered him a drink, though I grabbed something sweet and strong for myself.

"I wanted to apologize in person for last week," I said as Reuben made himself comfortable in his chair. "My past in the monster world is one of the reasons I'm here now, and sometimes, it affects me more than other times."

Reuben nodded in understanding. "I get that," he said softly. "We don't have to talk about anything you don't feel comfortable talking about."

"No, I... I'd like to," I said. "I don't usually talk about it, but I feel like you might be someone who can understand."

Reuben blinked in confusion but nodded. "All right," he offered.

"It's not very pleasant," I warned.

Reuben looked a little sad. I had a feeling he knew the gist of what was coming. "That's all right. I still would like to hear it."

I took a large swallow of my drink before I started.

"In the monster world, blue sea dragons like me are only one of many types of creatures that live in the water, and we are far from the largest or the scariest. We are predators, make no mistake, but our prey is usually fish and jellyfish, occasionally other smaller creatures found under or near the water.

"Several times a year, all of the blue sea dragons in the area wanting to reproduce are drawn to one singular location for a mating event. We're what I learned humans call 'hermaphrodites.' We have two sets of genitalia." I glanced up at Reuben to make sure I wasn't making him uncomfortable, but he was listening intently. "We always coupled multiple times with different dragons, so there was no way of knowing whose offspring was whose, as any of us could potentially carry a child. There never seemed to be a reason for one sea dragon to become pregnant over another. It didn't even matter which sets of genitals were used, 'cause they were connected within us, and both connected to a womb. Some had a preference of which type of genitals they used, but all were compatible, and all could produce offspring. We birth live young after nearly a year, though we only produce one pup at a time, maybe twins in a very rare instance, very much like humans do.

"During one of these mating events a number of years ago, I became pregnant. I had never been fully sure about being a parent, first-time jitters and all. But once my child was born, it was wonderful, better than I could have expected. Their name was Bogunn. They were so bright and inquisitive and... just perfect. We age similar to humans, and Bogunn was nine years old when I lost them."

Reuben inhaled softly, and I took the moment to pour more liquor into my glass.

"It happened really suddenly. A creature came up from the deep, with massive teeth and tentacles. Bogunn and I were separated, and before I could do more than find them in the chaos, the water around me turned red, and I tasted blood. I frantically looked for Bogunn, but the only thing I saw was the creature sinking back into the darkness below, one blue dragon fin sticking out from between its teeth."

"Oh my god," Reuben breathed softly. I knocked back my entire drink and refilled it without being aware that I had.

"If I could have died right there, or sacrificed myself for Bogunn, I would have. I dove down, hoping beyond hope that I could save them, but the creature descended too fast, and it disappeared even beyond where my swimming capabilities were able to take me. I never saw that creature again either. I don't even know what it was. I only know that it had taken from me the one thing I treasured most in my life."

Reuben had several tears running down his cheeks, and he reached over to place his hand on my arm. It was warm and heavy. "God, Glauruss, I'm so sorry." I swallowed the rest of my drink. Reuben squeezed my arm again. "I know a spouse is different than a child, but I understand the pain that... that comes with sudden loss."

"I know life is dangerous in the water, but it still felt as though it could never happen to me," I said. I did not have tear ducts, so I couldn't cry, but my skin heated as the emotions swirled inside of me like a hurricane. "That my child would be safe because they were so young and innocent. If anyone had died that day, it should have been me."

Reuben nodded slowly. "I understand that too. How a kind, good person can suddenly be gone. But your own child… I can't even imagine how that must feel, even after so long."

My head was starting to swim, and not in a good way. "I don't remember a lot from the days and weeks after it happened. I stopped eating and taking care of myself. I lost so much of my body weight that I could hardly stand to be in the water because it was so cold. I thought about just curling up on land somewhere and letting myself dry out entirely until I was nothing but bones."

Reuben gazed back at me with his deep, brown eyes. I was pretty sure he understood that too. His grief was still fresh. "Do you have days where you just don't even want to get out of bed?" I asked before I meant to. "Where you hope you just die in your sleep and not wake up again?"

"Yeah," Reuben said softly, squeezing my arm again. "Yeah, I've been feeling that a lot."

"Fuck, the things that some dragons said to me," I said, rubbing at my face with my free hand. "I was still young, I could have another child, like that would make everything better. Like there wasn't any risk of something like that happening a second time. At least by myself, if I was killed by another creature, it wouldn't be a huge loss to anyone."

I expected Reuben to respond with something trying to reassure me that that was not true, that everything would be all right, that I had so much to live for. But one glance up into his stricken face, and I knew he was feeling the exact same way. He knew that pain as much as I did, even if he had only been dealing with it for a few weeks instead of years.

And then my stomach revolted on me. Whatever amount of liquor I had had during my emotional ride, it was too much. I had to make a quick decision, and the balcony was closer than the bathroom. I dashed through the open cabin doors, catching myself on the railing as I leaned down and vomited. Hard. Liquid came out my mouth and my snout, burning and stinging. It felt like it might have even come out of my eyes. I realized with a jolt of shame that Reuben had followed me out and was standing just behind me. I vomited again, all of the alcohol in my body trying to evacuate itself as quickly as possible.

Chapter 8

Reuben

Glauruss didn't have hair that I needed to hold as he vomited over the side of the boat, but I still laid a hand on his back in reassurance. At least I had a strong stomach when it came to sick people, so him throwing up didn't make me feel sick. I was honestly not surprised it had happened. I don't think he realized how much he had drunk while he was telling me his story, and the emotions it must have brought up would have been difficult for anyone to deal with, even without so much alcohol in his system.

Once he was done and had straightened up against the railing, I rubbed his back. "You need a drink of water?"

"Please," he mumbled. I moved inside the cabin and over to the mini fridge to find a bottle of water and bring it back to him. He took it and sipped at it before turning to me. His eyes didn't have pupils, but I could tell he was looking deep into my own. "Fuck, I'm sorry."

I just gave him a small smile. "Feeling better?" Glauruss nodded, sipping at the water again, his gaze dropping to the deck beneath our feet. His legs were shaky. "Here, lean on me, let's go sit down," I said. He looked uncertain, as he was taller than me, but he draped one blue arm around my shoulders and let me lead him back into the cabin and over to his chair. He sank into it with a sound that sounded very much like he was trying to stifle a sob. I hadn't seen him cry yet, but I wasn't even sure if sea dragons *could* cry. It was obvious the story and the memories of it haunted him, the way my sorrow over losing Kyle was hovering over me like a storm cloud.

Unsure if he wanted me to be that close to him in the moment, I sat back down in the chair across from him again, resting my elbows on my knees. There were so many things I could say, but I wasn't sure if any of them would be helpful or even welcome, so I just stayed quiet until Glauruss finally lifted his head to look at me.

"I totally understand if you want to go," he said softly.

"Why would I want to go?" I asked, tipping my head a little.

"I probably made you super uncomfortable with all of that," he said, taking the tip of his tail in his hands and giving it a few nervous twists.

"I want to make sure you're okay," I said.

He nodded, dropping his eyes to the floor again. "I am. I'm fine."

I very much doubted that, but I wasn't about to contradict him.

"I don't even know... why I asked you to come back," Glauruss finally admitted, eyes still on the floor. "Why I felt like I needed to tell you all of that."

"Have you told anyone else in the human world?" I asked. He shook his head. "No."

I gave him a small smile, probably the same one people had been giving me for the past few weeks. "If there's one thing I've learned about grief recently, it's that it's very lonely. Even if you have friends or family, there's still a lot that goes on internally that others can't help with."

"You don't need the added burden of my sad story," Glauruss said, looking up at me then.

"You're not a burden," I said firmly. "Not any more than I am when I talked to you about Kyle."

Glauruss gave me a smile, a small one, but it held a spark of something that I thought might be hope. "Is it really all right if I talk about them?"

"Of course!" I said, my heart aching. "People seem afraid to talk about someone who died. It's a weird thing we humans do, we just don't acknowledge the dead, like that makes it all better. But it doesn't. It just makes things awkward." I barely knew Glauruss, but I knew that the hurt must be terrible for him, even after all this time. My own grief was like an open wound that just kept bleeding and stabbing me at moments when I least expected it. "Is thinking about Bogunn what drives you to drink?" I asked gently.

He nodded slowly. "Yes. I know it's not a great way to handle it, especially as a monster in the human world but... it makes the pain go away, just for a little while."

"I think we all deal with grieving in our own way," I said. "I've never been much of a drinker, but I understand that losing someone so precious to you so suddenly hurts like hell. And you'd give anything to make that pain go away."

Glauruss finished his water and leaned forward in his chair with his arms on his legs like I was. "Yes," he agreed softly. "Even just for that short time."

"Do you *like* feeling that way?" I asked. "Like what alcohol does to you?"

Glauruss looked crestfallen, gazing down at his feet. "I like the pain going away, but I don't like how I feel after. And I worry that I'm going to do something that will hurt someone, and I'll just be a monster. If I hurt someone, not only would I have to return to the monster world, but all monsters could be seen in a bad light."

As a black, gay man, I understood that feeling all too well too. "Do you want to stop drinking?" I asked, keeping my voice gentle. If he didn't, then nothing I would say would be helpful to him.

Glauruss hesitated, and I could see a blush coming to his

blue cheeks. He slowly lifted his pupil-less eyes to me. "Yes," he said softly.

"That's already half the battle right there," I said, trying to keep my voice cheerful but not so much that it sounded forced. "I can't say I'm an expert or anything, but I'm willing to help you as much as I can."

"Really?" Glauruss looked so hopeful, his head perking up, and there was a new light in his eyes.

"Really," I said. "There are resources out there. Meetings, counselors."

Glauruss looked a little uncertain as he gazed back at me. "Have you ever gone through something like that?" he asked.

"No," I admitted. "I was never much of a drinker, and my only drug use was some pot in college. Just wasn't really ever my thing. But I did work with at-risk teens when I was younger, and a lot of them had substance abuse problems, or risks for it. And I definitely can understand the appeal of trying to numb your memories and the grief that brings."

"Grief sucks," he said, and I let out a huff of laughter.

"It really does."

"It's going to be tough for a few days as your body gets used to not drinking. Do you have someone who can be with you?"

Glauruss' face fell. "No."

"It might be better for you to check yourself into the hospital," I said, not sure if he would be open to that idea or not. "They can help ease you through the worst of it, and I think they have some medicines that can help with the backlash."

He looked thoughtful for a moment before he nodded. "Will you come visit me there?"

I blinked at the sudden question. "I... Yes. Yes, I can do that. I can even take you there myself if you want."

"Wednesday?" Glauruss asked hopefully. "I have a rental Tuesday."

"I can take you Wednesday," I replied, giving his hand a squeeze.

I wasn't sure what would come of my offer to help Glauruss with his addiction as I headed home again. I supposed some part of it was pity for the sea dragon after what he went through, but, I realized, I didn't want to pity him, nor would pity be helpful. We shared a pain between us, a pain that not everyone could understand. The pain of losing someone close to us suddenly, violently, of having that hole suddenly punched in our hearts that just kept bleeding and bleeding no matter how much we tried to heal it. Helping him by supporting his recovery was something I could do that would give me a purpose and something to focus on other than myself. He would have to do most of the work himself, but I could at least be there to encourage him and hold his hand if he needed. Sometimes, that was enough.

Chapter 9

Glauruss

It was several years after losing Bogunn that I heard about these strange portals to another world that had been opening up, and monsters had already crossed over to this new place. What difference did it make to me if I was in this world or a different one? The risks associated with going into the unknown felt minimal compared to the sense of hope that I felt. I had been so lost, but perhaps I could find a purpose beyond the portal in this new world. And, if I did not, I gave myself permission to give up. Whatever dangers might lurk in this new world could have me, and I would not fight it.

It took a while for me to get settled into the human world at Gilmer Rock. Luckily, I was able to survive in both fresh and salt water, and the lake there provided a haven for the water-based creatures in the sanctuary town. I was required to have a job to stay in the human world, and when my ability to swim deeper than any normal human was discovered, I began to work with a construction company that specialized in underwater installations and restorations. Bridges, pipelines, tunnels, and even a few fancy-schmancy buildings along the beach. I was given special permission to travel with the construction company out of Gilmer Rock for specific projects, which I counted myself lucky for, as I got to see more of the human world than most monsters who had come through the portals.

What maybe wasn't so lucky was the fact that construction crews, when they are done for the day and have nowhere to be, tend to drink pretty heavily. As not only the newest member of the crew, but also a monster, my crewmates found it incredibly entertaining to see how many drinks they could get into me before I started acting foolishly. When I first started drinking, I did not know that alcohol caused inebriation. It didn't take long for them, and later me, to learn that I was just as susceptible to the effects of liquor as humans were. I thought, rather foolishly reflecting back on it, that my silly antics and outrageous statements were because I was having fun with these humans who were enjoying themselves. It was only after several nights of drinking, when I finally had so much that I ended up puking my guts out right there on the beach in front of everyone, that I learned how intoxicating alcohol was and the reaction it caused in my body, not dissimilar to my human friends.

I learned then that I needed to be more cautious about my drinking, but I didn't want to stop. For a short while, the pain was tolerable. Once in a while, I was even able to forget and let go. The pleasure alcohol brought when I was (what I thought was) responsible with it, outweighed the negatives. I often found myself drinking, even when I was not with my construction crew. Far too much. Having a blackout after stumbling into the ocean is not a good situation. More than once, I woke up to find myself underwater with no knowledge of how I got there and no idea where I was in relation to my home. The fact that I did not end up dead any of these multiple times was nothing short of miraculous.

In the monster world, life was unpredictable and dangerous, so a lot of monsters tended to live like every day was their last. Of course, I had learned that some humans did the same; their world may not have had as many immediate dangers as the monster world did, but it still held plenty of accidents and threats. I had to make sure I wasn't one of them.

One thing I had learned from my time in the human world was that when you looked different, like a monster, people would judge all monsters by you. Even if you knew almost no other monsters, or were new to the human world, you still represented all monsters when people met you. I had to be very cautious about everything I did. Which sucked. That's not to say I didn't want to be a decent monster-person, it was just exhausting having to always put up a polite front for people.

I had learned that grief was a lonely emotion, and it was made worse by the isolation and shame that alcohol caused. I was more than a little embarrassed that Reuben saw me that way. I would have completely understood if he had walked away, blocked me, and never spoken to me again. The fact that he had not only been concerned for me, but was even willing to help me was amazing. And, for some reason, I did not want to let him down. Maybe it was because he was going through the same feelings I had and was still managing to hold himself together, at least in public. I admired that.

I took my last drink Tuesday evening as I cleaned up my boat after my clients had gone home with their fishing catches. And then I poured out all of the liquor that was not part of the bar for the boat. I was ashamed of how much that was, how many half-empty bottles were lying around my bedroom. I really was lucky that I had not ever done anything unforgiveable or hurt someone. I knew that facing my own pain was going to suck. But I needed help. Reuben was willing to offer it. It was possible another opportunity like this might never present itself again. I had to take the helping hand.

Reuben picked me up early Wednesday afternoon after he took a half day off from work. I felt bad making him miss work just to take care of me, but he reassured me it was all right. "My boss is very understanding of needing time off to deal with things from Kyle." He said this without a change of tone or sadness in his eyes, the first time I had witnessed him say his spouse's name without reaction.

"I really do appreciate this," I said as I tried to make myself comfortable on his front seat. My tail was in the way, and I had to curl it awkwardly around me. "I want to be better."

He smiled at me. "I think you'll be able to do it," he said. "Wanting to change is powerful."

"I'm a little afraid," I confessed. I hadn't said those words to anyone before, and I wondered if he would think badly of me for it.

But instead, Reuben reached a hand over and squeezed my thigh in reassurance. We hadn't touched that often, so every time we did, it was like a wave of warm water brushing over my skin. "It's all right to be afraid. It's a scary situation. I was scared when Kyle died too. Having to face that pain, the unknown future… It's hard. And you know it's going to hurt, so your body and mind are trying to protect you however they can."

I smiled weakly and laid a hand overtop of his on my leg. "It's been years, and it still hurts like it was yesterday."

"I know," Reuben said softly, his fingers pressing into my skin in a comforting squeeze. And I was sure that he did.

Reuben helped get me checked in at the hospital. Everyone

there was exceptionally kind and professional. The first few days were a struggle. They gave me some medication that helped with my body detoxing after not drinking for several days. I got bad shakes and headaches. I probably would have soaked the bed in sweat if I had been able to sweat. I spent a lot of time in the shower to ensure I didn't dry out, and I had a constant supply of water to drink as well. One of the doctors even arranged for me to swim around the physical therapy pool. I had never been in a pool before. The chlorine made my skin a little itchy, but it was nice to be submerged again, and a shower cleared the itchiness away. I do not like thinking about how awful I felt those few days, and I was so relieved when the symptoms seemed to be lessening.

I texted Reuben on Saturday afternoon, after everything seemed to have cleared up. He came up to visit me that evening. "I wasn't sure if you liked flowers," he said as he walked in with a vase full of what I thought might be sunflowers. "But they always make me happy when I'm not feeling well."

I smiled. He was so sweet to even think of that at all when he had so much else going on. I wondered vaguely if he had been this thoughtful with Kyle as well. "Thank you, they're lovely."

Reuben set them on the window sill before sitting down in a chair next to the bed. "How are you feeling?"

I sighed. "You were right, those couple days were rough. But I do feel much better now. Finally starting to feel like my head is on straight."

Reuben smiled and took my hand, giving it a gentle squeeze. I hadn't expected him to touch me, but it was nice. I curled my wispy fingers around his hand. "Are you feeling good about being able to break your addiction?"

I nodded. "I think so. I don't want a repeat of that withdrawal again. That sucked so hard."

Reuben laughed one of his deep belly laughs. "I can only imagine. But at least that part's over."

"I'm definitely looking forward to getting back to the ocean," I commented. "I swam in the pool, but it's just not the same."

"And you don't get the nice ocean views with a pool," Reuben pointed out. "I've really enjoyed that from your boat."

I chuckled at that. "I love that too. I suppose I do get to see it more often than you do."

"Very much so. I live so close, but I hardly ever go to the beach," Reuben said thoughtfully.

"Why is that?" I asked, settling back against my pillow. "Just not a beach human?"

Reuben laughed. "I suppose. I've always been a bit more of a homebody. I like to travel if I'm going somewhere specific, but I've never been much of an outdoors kind of guy."

"Well, you'd have to be outdoors if you wanted to see me more," I said before realizing that I had just made it sound like we were going to be dating.

Reuben heard it too, his cheeks flushing in the fluorescent hospital lighting. "I suppose so."

"Sorry, I didn't mean for that to sound so... uh..."

"No. No, I... I get what you meant..." Reuben sounded so flustered, and he gazed up at me from under half-lidded eyes. "I, um... I know our relationship is kind of weird now, with... with Kyle being gone. But I guess it was always going to be a little weird, since we were planning to meet for a one-time threesome."

I nodded. It would be weird for me to proposition him now, and probably even weirder to proposition him when I was in a hospital bed. But I wasn't opposed to the idea of getting to know Reuben better either. He had been very kind and caring to me when he didn't have to. Even if we were just friends, he would be a good friend to have. "I know neither of us are really in a good place right now. But I have really enjoyed getting to know you, and I'd like the chance to know you more. As a friend."

Was it my imagination, or did his eyes flicker with just a hint of sadness? It was probably nothing. Reuben smiled and squeezed my hand gently. "I'd like to get to know you better. I think we both could use a friend right now who understands."

Both of us lapsed into silence for a few moments. Reuben actually spoke first, which surprised me. "I think one thing you should do is talk to Mike. He seems like a good guy who cares about you. If you let him know you don't want to drink anymore, he can look out for you if you come to the bar."

I flushed a bit at that. I supposed I would consider Mike my friend, but it still felt awkward to think about telling people about my addiction. I knew in the human world that there were a lot of addictions that people could and did have. But it also was not something that a lot of people chose to talk publicly about. There was a strange stigma surrounding addiction, like it was a moral failing of some kind. And I knew it was hard for people to admit to things they were embarrassed or ashamed about. Even though I came from a different world, I had picked up on that shame during my time in this one. Plus, it was Mike's job to give people alcohol. Would he really take so kindly to me telling him I didn't want to drink anymore? "You think so?"

Reuben nodded. "Yeah, I do. You don't have to go super deep into it or anything. But he's your friend, I bet he'll understand."

I had very few friends in this world, but I did count Mike in that number. Reuben had been kind and compassionate. Mike was more of a hard-ass, but he also was a good guy, one of the few humans I fully trusted. "Okay," I agreed, giving Reuben a closed-lip smile. "Thank you. And thank you for helping me with this. It... I didn't know what to do."

Reuben squeezed my hand again. "It's hard. I get that. But you're taking the right steps to make things better for yourself."

"I'm sorry I'm making you deal with this when you've got so much else on your plate," I said.

"Hey, stop that," he scolded gently. "I wouldn't deal with it if I didn't want to help. And I know you can do this. You're strong. Stronger than you think. And I'm going to help you so you don't fall."

Chapter 10

Reuben

My thoughts on the conversation Glauruss and I had had in the hospital kept circling my mind like a whirlpool as I dropped him off at the beach on Sunday evening after he was released in good health. We had agreed to be friends, which made sense for where we both were. And what I had said was true; I wouldn't help him if I couldn't handle it. Kyle was gone, but the pieces of his life were slowly slotting into place. Death was final. I couldn't 'fix' it. But Glauruss was something I could help with. I didn't kid myself that I could 'fix' him. But I could support him in what would be a difficult journey and help him live a better life. The living still had to live after the dead were gone.

That brought up more thoughts in my mind. I was fifty-one. I wasn't a completely old dog yet, though sometimes my body decided otherwise. But I didn't have to entirely give up on the idea of romance or relationships just because Kyle was gone. I hopefully still had another twenty to thirty years left in me, but I also didn't necessarily have good health for all of them either. Perhaps my mind would go like my dad's, or I'd get some long-lasting disease like my momma. I wasn't necessarily planning to find romance again, but who knew what would happen? I liked Glauruss. More than I had realized. It could be and probably was trauma bonding, sharing our pain with one another and connecting on a deeper level because of it. But that wasn't necessarily bad. As long as we both wanted the same thing. When he had said he wanted us to be friends, something inside of me had tugged just a bit. I knew friendship was better right now. He had to get through his recovery, and I was still only a few weeks into mourning Kyle.

My phone buzzed in my pocket. I pulled it out and saw that it was the care center where my dad was. A sense of dread came over me as I answered. I took a deep breath. "Hello?"

"Mr. Thompson?"

"Speaking."

"Hi, this is Jenny over at Scottdale Memory Care." The nurse on the line sounded so gentle, I knew what the next few words would be before she spoke them out loud. "I'm afraid your father, Benjamin, passed away this afternoon."

I waited for the freeze, the cold, the shaking, the anxiety. Any of the reactions I had had when I received the news about Kyle. But they didn't come. All I felt was a sort of calm peacefulness wash over me. My father was with my mother now. He wasn't suffering or confused anymore. And I was an orphan. That felt strange to think at fifty-one years old, but that was the word for it. Both of my parents were gone.

"Mr. Thompson?"

I realized I hadn't answered her. "I'm here, sorry. Thank you for your call, Jenny. I'll call my sister, and then arrange for the funeral home to pick him up."

I called Brenda. I heard her stifle sobs that sounded very much like the ones that had come out of me when I got the news about Kyle. I knew the pain she was going through. "I'll pack a bag and come over there," I said. There was going to be a lot to do to prepare for another funeral and to close my dad's affairs, though certainly not as many as I had had to do for Kyle. I had to be the strong one now.

I packed a suitcase, called my boss, thankful again for his understanding, and then I texted Glauruss.

Chapter 11

Glauruss

I WAS RELEASED FROM the hospital on Sunday late afternoon with a plan to attend some addiction group meetings via computer and a once a week one-on-one with a counselor to check in. Reuben picked me up in his car and took me back to the beach. I had never learned to drive and probably wouldn't. My feet were very large and more designed for swimming than for driving. I offered for him to come sit with me for a while, but he told me he had to get home to take care of some things. "But I do want to see you again soon," he said, giving me that sweet smile that I was learning to love. "And if you feel like you might fall off the wagon, call me anytime, day or night. I'm here for you."

I did several loops around my boat, making sure that every bit of liquor that was not for my business had been poured out. Then I went for a long swim, which helped to clear my head. I walked up onto the beach near the boardwalk as the sun was just about to dip below the horizon. Mike was at his stand, and I remembered Reuben's prompt about talking to Mike. Now seemed as good a time as any. The final patrons were wandering off as I sat down on a stool, flicking my tail out of the way. "Hey, Mike."

"Hey, Blue!" Mike greeted me as he grabbed a couple dirty glasses from off the counter. "Fruit punch or tropic storm?"

I held up my hand. "Actually, I wanted to talk to you about that."

Mike looked a little worried. "Am I losin' my touch?"

I chuckled. "No, no, your touch is great. Too great. I, uh… I'm quitting drinking," I said.

Mike gazed at me for a long moment, then nodded solemnly. "I get it," he said softly.

"You do?" I asked, tipping my head curiously.

He nodded again. "I've known you for a while now, mate. I was gettin' a little worried about you." I felt simultaneously guilty and also relieved. I didn't want Mike to worry about me; he was a good guy. But if he recognized that I had a problem too, I had made the right decision to stop drinking. "Is it cause of that guy? Reuben?"

"Oh," I said, giving him a small grin. "You noticed him."

"I'm a bartender," Mike said by way of explanation, which probably made more sense to him than it did to me.

"Yeah, I… I really like him, Mike. I think I told you

that he lost his husband recently?" Mike nodded in acknowledgement. "We got to talking, and… I didn't like what drinking was doing to me. I was using it to dull the pain from… some stuff in the past, and it wasn't healthy."

Mike gave me a knowing look. "You gotta do what's best for you. Fuckin' yourself up might feel like an answer, but it's usually not. You gonna see more of that guy?"

I flushed a bit. "Yeah, maybe? I don't think either of us are in a good place to have like a full-on relationship right now. But I think we both could use a friend."

"I get that too," Mike said. "Just see where things lead."

"Exactly," I said, my eyes drifting over the bar to the maraschino cherries sitting in their little plastic bin. "I'm gonna miss your cherries though."

Mike chuckled. "Hey, just cause I ain't servin' you alcohol don't mean you can't have cherries. Here, lemme mix you something, see if you like it." He turned away, grabbing a few things. I watched him curiously. Mike's smoothness in mixing was an art, and I always enjoyed it. He set down a highball glass in front of me with a reddish-pink bubbly drink over ice, and several cherries speared onto a cocktail stick, just the way I liked. "Here. Shirley Temple. Classic nonalcoholic drink."

I took the glass and swallowed a mouthful. "Holy shit, Mike," I said, crunching some of the ice between my sharp teeth. "That's amazing!"

"Super simple, I can whip ya up one any time you want,"

Mike said with a smile.

I nodded and swallowed the rest of the glass in one gulp, ice and all, then ate the cherries off the stick one by one. "I'd like that."

"I got you, Blue," he said, flashing me another smile. "Takes a lot of guts to admit when you got a problem. I've been there myself."

"You were addicted to alcohol?" I asked, glancing around the bar that surrounded him.

"Nah. Heroine. Bad stuff, it will fuck you up pretty good. And I lost everything because of it. My wife left me, took my daughter and son. I only hear from them once a year at Christmas now." Mike's brown eyes took on a faraway look. "I finally got clean about six years ago, relapsed a few times before that. They're grown now, and I'm hopin' I can rebuild those relationships with my kids. But I screwed 'em up pretty bad, so I don't blame 'em if they decide they don't wanna have anything to do with their old man."

That had to be difficult, having family who was alive who wanted nothing to do with him, I thought. But as long as they were alive, there was still hope. "What are their names?" I asked.

"Maggie and Michael Jr.," Mike said with a chuckle. He dug in his pocket and pulled out his wallet, flipping it open to a picture of two smiling kids that was obviously many years old. Maggie had long, blond hair and was holding a black and white kitten to her chest. Michael Jr. was next to her, giving the camera a wide, cheesy grin to show off his missing top front teeth.

"They're beautiful," I said, feeling my eyes burn with sudden tears.

"Yeah," Mike agreed, giving the picture a fond look before putting the wallet back in his pocket. He cleared his throat. "So, uh... Another Shirley Temple?"

"Yeah. I'm gonna need like three more of those after all that sentimental stuff," I said with a grin, and Mike let out a guffaw of laughter as he began to mix.

When I got back to my boat, there was a text from Reuben, which surprised me. I hadn't expected to hear from him so soon. But my heart sank when I read the message.

My dad passed away today. Going to my sister's for the week to get things settled. I'll be back later this week, but call me if you need to talk.

Even when dealing with another crisis, he was still kind and sweet and caring about others. I texted him back.

Im so sorry! Take care. I'll be ok I told Mike. Lmk when you're back in town.

He sent me a thumbs up in response, and I left it on 'read.' He had enough to deal with right now. I could at least be respectful of his time and be there for him when he returned.

Chapter 12

Glauruss

I HEARD FROM REUBEN several times during the week as he texted updates. His father's funeral was going to be on Thursday, he would be home Saturday. Even in the midst of what I was sure was dealing with his own grief and his family, he still asked me how I was doing. I told him I had not had any alcohol and that I was doing well. The first part was the truth. The second part was a lie.

Having to face my memories hurt. It hurt like fucking hell. I missed the safety net that drinking had brought. I wanted to curl up and not think about how much I missed my child, even so many years after their passing.

I sent Reuben a text on Thursday, just telling him I was thinking about him and wishing for peace for him and his family. He hearted my comment but didn't respond. I was sure he was very busy.

I tried to distract myself as much as I could. I swam for hours, diving so deep into the ocean that I nearly suffocated myself. So deep, as if I might find Bogunn there. So deep that it was like I was the only creature in the entire ocean. Vast, cold, empty, and completely alone. The water was my mind, my mind was the water; I didn't even know where the water ended and I began. I could just let go. The pain would go away. But then I wondered, if I died, would Reuben cry for me? He had already lost so much. Even if I was just his friend, I couldn't do that to him.

I didn't get out of the water until long after the sun had set. I headed straight for the bar on my boat and grabbed a bottle of vodka. I broke the seal on it and pulled off the cap.

And then I stopped. I wasn't going to make it better. I heard Reuben's voice. *"I know you can do this. You're strong. Stronger than you think. And I'm going to help you so you don't fall."*

It was so late. Reuben would be back tomorrow. Surely, I could wait? He had been through so much, and I didn't need to make it worse with my problems. It felt selfish to want to talk to him when I knew what he was dealing with. But his words rang in my mind. *"Call me anytime, day or night. I'm here for you."* The vodka bottle was still in my hand. I set it down, turned, and walked out onto the deck. My hands shook a little as I pulled out my phone. "Call Reuben," I prompted it.

Reuben's name came across the screen as I turned it onto speaker. It rang several times, and then it went to voicemail. I decided not to leave one. He had enough to contend with right now. He didn't need to be part of my pity party; I would just deal with this alone. And then my phone began to ring. Reuben was calling me back. Surprised, I answered, "Hello?"

"Hey," Reuben said, his voice warm. "Sorry, my phone was in the other room, and it went to voicemail before I could grab it."

I suddenly realized how stupid it was for me to call Reuben just because I was having emotions. He didn't need that kind of pressure while he was still grieving. "I'm sorry. You're with your family," I said. "We can talk another time."

"It's okay," Reuben said, surprisingly gentle. "What's up? Is everything all right?"

"I'm all right. I'm sorry. I shouldn't have called."

"Honey." The pet name froze me instantly. I wasn't even sure if he was aware he said it. "Obviously you felt like you needed to talk. What is it?"

"I..." I swallowed hard. Reuben was very perceptive; I supposed the least I could do was make it worth bothering him. "I'm sorry, I'm just... having a rough night. Struggling."

"Do you need me to come over?"

The question shocked me. "No, you don't have to do that!" I said quickly. "It's the middle of the night, and you're hours away."

"Fuck that," he said, and that actually made me chuckle just a little. Reuben didn't swear often, so when he did, it was always well-timed. "I was going to leave in the morning anyway. Are you on your boat?"

"Yeah."

"Let me say goodbye and load up my suitcase, and then I'll come right there."

"You really don't have to do that," I said quickly.

"Glauruss." My name on his lips sounded stern. I could almost see his brown eyes gazing pointedly at me. "I want to do this. I'll be there as soon as I can."

"Okay," I said.

"Okay, see you soon." He hung up. I stared at the phone in my hand. I had called him in the middle of the night, when he was with his sister after his father's funeral, and he was driving home just to check on me. It wasn't what I had expected, but it also sent a warmth flooding through me. He cared enough about me to come check on me in person. That was more than most people or other monsters would do for me. I went for another swim.

It was a few hours before Reuben pulled up in his car, parking in the lot and walking along the pier. I stepped out onto the dock to wait for him, and he lifted his hand in a wave as he approached. He was wearing a pair of sweatpants, a tee-shirt, and a hoodie, as well as his flip-flops that made slapping sounds against his heels as he approached me. "Hey," he said when he was close enough to not yell.

"Hi," I greeted back. "Thank you for coming. You really didn't have to come all this-"

He suddenly leaned in and gave me a gentle squeeze around the hips. "Hush. Let me decide what I do and do not have to do. It's a nice night. You wanna go sit on the deck?"

"You read my mind," I chuckled, crossing the short gangplank back onto the boat and then holding out my hand to assist him. He stepped cautiously onto the plank, then down into the boat, using my hand to brace himself.

"Everything moving under me still gets me every time," he said with a small smile on his lips. They looked shiny in the moonlight, and I could smell his pomegranate chapstick.

I chuckled, letting him still hold onto my hand. It felt nice in mine. "I hardly notice it anymore, but when I step onto land, it always takes a few moments to readjust."

He laughed, the sound bright in the stillness of the night around us, the only other sounds being the soft crash of waves and the hollow clunk of boats bobbing where they were anchored at the pier. I motioned to two of the deck chairs on the back of the boat, facing the open water. He moved over to one, still holding my hand, and then dragged it over a few feet until it was side by side with another one. "There, perfect."

I grinned, sinking into one as he held my hand and sat in the other, squirming around until he was comfortable. "All right. Talk to me. What's going on?"

I sighed and stared out at the inky black water, its waves

crested with shining silver moonlight. "I just got to thinking. About Bogunn, and family. And that started pushing me down a road I didn't want to go down."

"Were you wanting to drink?" Reuben asked, no judgement in his voice, just calm concern.

"Yes," I said honestly. "But I didn't. I called you."

"Good," he said, giving my hand a squeeze. "I'm proud of you, honey!"

That startled me. I don't think anyone had ever told me they were proud of me before. "I really didn't mean for you to come back early," I said by way of trying to cover my embarrassment.

Reuben shook his head. "I wouldn't offer if I didn't mean it." He sat up a little and held my hand tighter. "That's what I'm here for, to be here when you need someone to talk to."

I gazed back at him in the moonlight. He looked so sincere, so hopeful. I had only known Reuben for a short time, but I already knew that seeing him happy was important to me. He had been through so much, and I knew that him having to be there for me was adding to his stress. "I'm still sorry. I want to be the last one to let you down. I really appreciate you being here for me."

Reuben gave my hand another squeeze. "I'm happy to help, honey. Did you want to talk? About Bogunn or anything in particular?"

"I don't think I do," I said honestly. "I think just talking to you, giving my mind something else to focus on, helped a lot."

"Good," Reuben said gently. "We can talk about whatever you want. Or, we can just sit here and enjoy the night and the ocean."

"How did everything go with your family?" I asked.

"Good," he said with a sigh. "Pretty smooth, all things considered. A few more papers to file and whatnot, but Brenda's on it."

"Is it hard, having to say goodbye to your father so soon after losing Kyle?" I asked, unsure if this question would do more harm than good.

Reuben was silent for a moment before he replied, "I said goodbye to my dad a long time ago. His mind has been not good for years. I... I'm honestly kind of relieved that it's over."

"I suppose knowing that it will happen but not knowing when was difficult."

"Yeah," Reuben said. "We never know how long we have. I know that's why life is so precious. Because it ends. We have to make the most of the time we have."

That made something well in my throat, and I swallowed it. "Reuben?"

"Yeah?" he asked, turning to me curiously.

"I... I would very much like to kiss you."

Chapter 13

Reuben

"I would very much like to kiss you."

Glauruss' words were only slightly louder than the thunk of waves against the hull of the boat. I stared back at him, my heart picking up in my chest. Glauruss was still holding my hand, and he pulled it away, holding his hands up. "But not if you don't want it."

Glauruss' mottled, blue skin seemed to glow in the moonlight, making him look almost ethereal. I wondered if he looked like that underwater too when the sunlight touched him. I rose to my feet as I took a deep breath. I extended my hand to help him out of his chair. He took it, rising up until he was taller than me once more.

I know I moved first, because I was wondering how it would work with him not having lips. I took the sides of his jaw in between my hands, leaned in, and pressed a kiss to the lower part of his snout. I wasn't sure if he could feel it or if I had done it right, but he inhaled softly and nuzzled back against my cheek. His snout was slick, but I could feel the strength behind it.

"Reuben," he rumbled softly, and I could feel the vibrations against my neck. They traveled like fire licking up paper, through my arms, my torso, down between my legs. I felt desire there, warm and growing. I kissed him again, firmer this time. His arms went around me, his slick tentacle-like fingers pressing against my back as he held me close. I felt the beat of his heart against my own. I missed that feeling. I missed being touched.

"Take me to bed," I said softly.

He looked down at me in surprise. "Are you sure?"

"Yes," I said. "Please. I... I need this."

He nodded and took both of my hands in his, guiding me to where a short stairwell went down. At the bottom was a door marked 'Private.' He opened it, flicked on the light, and led me inside.

The bedroom was small, the queen-size bed taking up most of the room in it. There was a shelf of books, a nightstand with the lamp on it that illuminated the small space, and a small TV mounted in one corner. There was a door leading to what I assumed was the bathroom.

Glauruss smiled, his teeth showing through just a bit. "I'm sorry it's not much."

I shook my head. "It's great," I said, kissing him again. I didn't care what it looked like. I just wanted to be with him. I realized that I was the only one with clothes on here. I slid off my flip-flops, then my hoodie. My t-shirt came off next, leaving me bare-chested. Glauruss' hands slid up, over the curves of my chest, down my stomach, following the little dark hairs. His fingers explored my skin, tracing the stretch marks and the rough patches with what almost felt like reverence. "I want to see all of you," he murmured.

I reached down and slid both my sweatpants and my boxers down together, stepping carefully out of them. I was now standing naked by his bed, my heart racing, sure that he could hear it in the small space. "Is this all right?" he asked.

"Yes," I said softly.

"I want to taste you."

That request made me flush a little. I sat down on the edge of the bed. Glauruss lowered himself to his knees between my spread thighs, his fluttery fingers still tracing over my skin, as if following the lines of a map. He leaned in, his breath hot on my inner thighs. He slid his snout down, the cool top of it settling under my belly to lift it away from my cock that was now at full arousal. His tongue slid out and ran up the underside of my cock, making me shiver. His tongue was thick and long, and he wrapped it around me with surprising dexterity. It felt so good; I mumbled some nonsense sounds that neither one of us understood.

"Lie back, and put your legs on my shoulders," he

instructed.

I did as he said, lifting my legs up to drape over his shoulders and down his slick back. He slid his tongue down and lapped at my hole, making me squirm. "Do you like that?" he asked.

"Yes," I said. He swirled his tongue around several more times before his tongue moved over my balls, and then back up to encase my cock. One of his hands slid between my legs, and two of his fingers brushed over my hole. They were soft like feathers, the touches light and teasing, but I could still feel the strength behind them. His tongue stroked up and down over my cock as his fingers stroked and teased over me, not pressing in, just stimulating me and sending little bolts of pleasure through me. I knew I wasn't going to last long like this as his other hand came up to squeeze lightly at my balls. "I... I'm gonna come," I warned him, my fingers digging into the sheets beneath me.

His fingers and tongue only pressed harder, and I lost myself with a gasping cry of pleasure. His tongue rolled and lapped over me, cleaning up every drop as my cock pulsed with delicious overstimulation.

He finally pulled back, leaving me gasping on the bed like a landed fish. He carefully helped me lower my legs to the bed, stroking over my thighs with his soft hands. "Do you want more, baby?"

The pet name made me smile as I peeked open my eyes to gaze back at him. "I wanna make you feel good too. Join me?" I patted the spot next to me.

He nuzzled his snout into my knee before smiling, just the smallest hint of his sharp teeth showing. I slid back on the bed and shifted so I was lying on my back with my head on the pillow. Glauruss slid next to me, plastering his body against my side as one of his hands caressed up and down my chest and stomach.

He was surprisingly warm; I realized that he probably was a warm-blooded creature or at least could control his body temperature in some way, if he was used to diving into the cold, deep waters. His skin against mine was almost satiny, slick and smooth. A few areas had a rough feel to them, not quite scales, and nothing sharp besides his teeth. He was a sleek creature of the water, to be sure.

"I would like to see you, if that's all right," I said with a soft chuckle, my eyes dropping a little below his waist. I had never seen a monster's dick before, let alone one who had two sets of genitals.

Glauruss laughed and nuzzled my neck before he sat up onto his knees. In between his legs was a small, smooth mound that reminded me of a Ken doll. I thought perhaps it would split open, so I was a little shocked when the mound actually folded upward, like lifting a door on a hinge. He seemed to tuck it into itself to keep it from coming down again. He did indeed have two sets of genitals, his erect cock coming from the top of the slit that seemed to be labial folds. He wasn't overly large, a very average human size and shape, which I was a surprisingly grateful for, having imagined monsters to have ridiculous-sized dicks. He ran his hand down his cock, and I could see that it was sticky with natural lubrication.

"Can I touch it?" I asked curiously.

Glauruss nodded, and I sat up, reaching one hand to run up the underside of his dick, then over the head before sliding down again, dipping one finger in between the soft, damp folds, watching to make sure I didn't do anything that hurt him. He just sighed in pleasure as my hand explored and stroked. "Do you have a preference of which you like to use?" I asked. He had told me some sea dragons had preferences.

He stroked a hand down my face, his fingertips curling in ways that normal fingers could not. "I prefer to use my dick, but I am happy to use either. Do you have a preference in bed?"

I flushed a little. "I... I actually prefer to be the bottom."

He nuzzled into my neck again. "Perfect. What position is most comfortable for you to be in?"

The question surprised me, though it probably shouldn't have. Kyle knew my preferences in bed from our years together. Being with a new partner who didn't know my body that way was going to take some getting used to, but I appreciated very much that he asked. "I actually really like being on my side," I said. "If that works."

He nodded and gave my cheek a nuzzling kiss. "Absolutely. Do what you need to do."

I rolled onto my side, adjusting my stomach and hips until everything rested comfortably, curling up my right knee to open myself up a little more. Glauruss' wispy fingers dipped again in between my butt cheeks, and I could feel now that they were covered with something slick, probably his natural lube. One finger squirmed inside of me, so soft and flexible that it didn't even twinge or burn. I moaned softly. "Yes..."

"Not hurting?" Glauruss asked.

"Not hurting," I echoed back. I could feel the finger fluttering inside of me in a strange sensation I had never felt before. It tickled and teased, creating a feeling almost like an itch I couldn't scratch as a second finger slid inside. I moaned again, my eyes closing at the delightful feeling. Despite having two fingers inside of me, they were so flexible and thin that it barely felt like fingers at all. "More," I pleaded softly.

Glauruss laughed and nuzzled the back of my neck as a third finger slid inside of me, the ends curling to press against my inner walls. I gasped, my right arm moving up to grab his shoulder behind me. "All right?" Glauruss asked.

"Yeah. Really good," I said. The fingers all moved differently inside of me, and my cock gave a little pulse between my legs, having recovered from my earlier orgasm. "Damn, that feels so good."

"Should I make you come from this?" Glauruss asked, giving my shoulder an ever-so-gentle nip with his teeth.

"No," I said, even though the idea was very appealing. "I

want you inside of me."

Glauruss nuzzled my shoulder, his fingers slowly sliding out of me. "Let me know if you need to stop."

I nodded, my arm around his neck letting go so I could grip the pillow lightly. He lifted my curled right leg and draped it over his hip as I felt the head of his cock press against me, much firmer than his fingers had been. I breathed out, and the head pushed inside of me. I gasped, my leg squeezing on his. "All right?" he asked, stroking a hand down my chest again.

"Yes," I said, tipping my head back under his chin. "Just go slow."

He did, pressing his hips forward to slide further, opening me up around his cock that was also that silky sleekness of the rest of him. When he was all the way inside of me, his front plastered against my back, I let out a sigh of pleasure. The slight stretch and burn were familiar but also different; the shape and size were a little smaller than Kyle, but not unpleasant. His snout brushed over my back, up and down my neck and shoulders. "Doing all right?" he asked, his voice a low thrum.

"Yes," I said, squirming a little to get my right hip comfortable, which made him hiss softly in pleasure as I shifted around him.

"Mmm, fuck, you feel so good, baby," he murmured in my ear, the tip of his tongue brushing out to tickle the back of it. That made me laugh; my ears had always been a little sensitive. I could feel his smile as he stroked his tongue over my ear playfully, making me squirm again, writhing against his hips.

"Can I move?" he asked me, one hand stroking over my hip and then curling to rest on my stomach.

"Yes," I moaned.

He began to roll his hips back and forth, his silky cock sliding back and forth inside of me. I could feel the wetness from his natural lube against the bottom of my butt cheeks as he moved. He started slow, stroking his hand over my chest and stomach, his flexible fingers curling around my nipples to caress them lightly, making my hips buck. I slid my hand down to my own cock, giving it a squeeze before starting to stroke myself as Glauruss rocked his hips into mine, faster now. "Yes, baby," he purred, giving my ear a little nip. "Just like that."

His cock sliding in and out of me felt so good, I didn't want it to end. His hand running over my chest, hips, stomach, every touch so soft and loving, was all I wanted in this moment. He growled softly as he began to move faster, his hips slapping against mine with a wet sound in the dim room. My hand followed the speed, and within a few moments, I was coming, crying out in pleasure as I spilled over my own hand, my body clenching around him, which only made the pleasure spike more as he continued to thrust hard and fast into me, panting in my ear. His own hips bucked, and he let out a shout, releasing himself inside of me. I lay on my side still, twitching and shivering as my body processed the sensations, pulses of pleasure traveling over me as my body tightened and relaxed around him.

I sighed softly in pleasure, my eyes drifting closed as I basked in his touch on my skin. And then, I began to cry.

Chapter 14

Glauruss

I RAN MY HAND down Reuben's chest. Reuben's body was soft and squishy in places, and I enjoyed the feel of his body against mine. My cock still pulsed inside of him for a moment as I came down from my own orgasm. Then I felt him take a deep, shuddery breath, and Reuben began to cry. Fat, hot tears rolled down his cheeks, and I instantly felt like I had kicked a puppy. "Hey, what's wrong?" I asked, reaching up to brush some of the tears away with my thumb, the feather-soft tip of my finger drifting over his cheek.

He took a large gulp of air that almost sounded like he was choking as he struggled to stop the tears. I didn't want him to feel like he couldn't cry around me. So, I just wrapped my arms around him and held him back against me, making soft soothing noises that I hoped didn't sound too much like growling to him. I nosed at his neck lightly, a few of his tears dripping over my snout. I carefully moved my hips so I slid out of him, but he didn't move away. He just curled back into my arms into a more comfortable position as he hugged my arms tightly to him.

He struggled for a moment to try to speak, and I just held him close, willing to wait as long as I needed to for him to get out everything that he was feeling. "I'm sorry," he finally said as he scrubbed at his eyes with a large hand.

I shook my head. "For what? You don't have to be sorry about anything."

He took a deep, shuddering breath before I felt the tension ease out of him. "I didn't mean to cry."

"Fuck that," I said, nosing lightly at his neck again. "I just don't want to hurt you."

"You didn't," he reassured me, stroking a hand up my arm. "You didn't. It was... It was just different." Reuben swallowed, and I watched his Adams' apple bob. "I... I'm sorry."

I frowned slightly. "For what?"

Reuben flushed, and I could see his round cheeks going red in the dimness, even with his back to me. "I don't... think I'm ready for this."

I inhaled softly. "Shit, I'm sorry! I didn't mean to push you!"

"No!" Reuben said quickly, sitting up rather suddenly. He turned to me as I sat up too. He took my hand in both of his and gave it a squeeze. "No, honey. You didn't. It's nothing you did."

I gazed back at him in the darkness. His eyes were on mine, and he looked so sorrowful. We were both silent for a long minute, neither seeming to know what to say, before Reuben finally murmured, "I thought I was ready to try and move on. But I'm not."

His words hurt me in a way that I was not expecting. It took me a moment to realize why. "I'm not asking you to move on," I said softly. "Please don't. I never want you to forget Kyle." He looked up at me, dark eyes confused. I tried to clarify. "I don't ever want to take his place. You have a lifetime of memories and experiences together. You and I... what we have, what we might have in the future, will be different. It will never be what you and Kyle had, no matter how much we care about each other. And that's all right."

"Is it really?" he asked softly, squeezing my hands. "I don't want you to ever feel like you're not important."

"Reuben," I said gently, and his worried eyes softened. "I'm not Kyle, and I don't want to be. If you want to keep seeing me, as lovers or just friends or whatever, that's enough for me. I don't need to be your one and only, or to be 'better' than what you had."

Reuben gazed back at me for a long moment before he lifted his hand and stroked my jaw, pressing a kiss to my snout before resting his forehead against it. "I do want to keep seeing you," he said softly. "I just don't know else I want. I still feel lost."

I wrapped my arms around him and hugged him to my chest. "That's all right. We don't need answers right now. Get some sleep, okay?"

As he laid by my side in the dark, my thoughts drifted once more to Bogunn. I would always miss them and love them and regret that I did not have more time with them. And I was sure Reuben would feel the same way about Kyle. I couldn't remember where I had heard it, but someone once said, "The hole they leave in your heart never goes away. Your heart just gets bigger as you fill it with more love." And I knew that would be the case. There would always be an emptiness in our hearts, and sometimes we would be sad or angry. And that was all right. We would be all right too.

Chapter 15

Reuben

I wasn't sure how I felt about being single. I had spent so many years living with people that I realized I had never really taken the opportunity to figure out who I was without someone. I had lived with my parents through high school, had a roommate during my college years, and then Kyle and I moved in together when I graduated and got my first apartment. We had been together ever since. I had never lived on my own, been able to make choices that only affected me. Being on my own was quiet and lonely sometimes. But other times, it was strangely relaxing. I was learning to make my own decisions. Even simple ones like what I wanted for dinner or what I wanted to watch on TV felt different when I didn't have to consider another person in the decision.

At the same time, I had seen the devastation my father

went through when my mother died. My mother had been his whole world, and when he was on his own, it seemed like he had lost the spark that he had once had, the excitement and enjoyment of life. He had been lost and didn't have a lot to look forward to. I didn't want that to be me. I knew I would grieve Kyle the rest of my life, but that didn't mean that I couldn't live without him. I, hopefully, had plenty of years left in me, and I knew that Kyle would not want me to be lonely in that time.

Glauruss and I sat on the deck of his boat, the sun shining down on us as we sipped mocktails. "I don't know that I'm ready to settle down with someone again," I blurted out. I felt awful as soon as the words left my mouth, and I fully expected Glauruss to get angry or at least be hurt by my words.

But instead, he nodded serenely. "I understand. You've been through a lot in a short amount of time. I'm sure it's a lot to process."

"It is," I said softly. "I just don't want you to feel like you have to hold yourself back if you want something more."

Glauruss looked surprisingly serious. "What I want is happiness for us both. That doesn't mean we have to be constantly together. We can still have a relationship even if we're not living together or married or anything."

"Is that really all right with you?" I asked. "Until we both know what we want?"

"That's one great thing about life," Glauruss said, his eyes crinkling into a bit of a smile. "We can decide what works for us. Our relationship doesn't have to look like anyone else's."

I realized that was very true. No one said we had to live together, get married, and ride a white horse happily ever after into the sunset. Right now, our happily ever after looked like two people, each living their own lives. We could sit together, talk, enjoy each other's company and bodies, and then we could each go to our separate homes. Just because there was physical distance between us did not mean that we were not in a committed relationship. We were beautifully broken by memories and pain, held together by love and companionship. Whatever the future held for us, we could decide what we wanted together. We still had life to live, and we were going to live it.

Epilogue

Glauruss

"Hey, guys!" Mike called and waved us over. My fingers tightened around Reuben's as we crossed the sand over to the beachside bar. Standing next to Mike was a stunning young woman with blond hair and a very round belly. "I want you to meet my daughter, Maggie," he said. "Maggie, Glauruss and Reuben. Glauruss, Reuben, Maggie. She came for a visit and to show me this!" He held up an odd-looking picture. "My first grandbaby, little Sophia!"

"Congratulations!" I said to Mike with a grin, then turned to Maggie. "And to you too, ma'am."

She giggled and tossed her hair. "Thank you, Mr. Glauruss. My dad has told me a lot about you."

"I deny everything," I said, shooting Mike a playful, stern look.

Reuben smiled softly at the picture. "That's so exciting! I hope we get to see her once she's born."

Maggie nodded, handing Reuben the picture, and he held it reverently. "We'll be sure to come visit. Do you live around here too, Mr. Reuben?"

"Oh, please, just Reuben is fine," he said, handing the photo back. "I live a little further inland, but Glauruss and I are seeing each other, so I'm out here pretty often."

"Oh, that's so nice!" Maggie said, glancing between us. "You two are really cute together."

Reuben blushed at that. He really was just the sweetest.

"Michael Jr. and I have been talking by email," Mike said. "He ain't quite ready to meet in person yet, but he says maybe when he comes home from college in a few months."

"That's great, Mike," I said, giving him a pat on the back. I nodded at Maggie. "Very nice to meet you."

"You too!" she said.

Reuben beamed at me as we walked to the dock with my boat. "I'm so glad Mike finally contacted his family, and that they are giving him a chance to make amends."

"Me too," I agreed. "He's a good guy."

We stepped onto the Dragon U2C Stuff. Reuben stood by my side as I drove the boat out into open water. We were going to do some deep-sea fishing. I hoped we'd catch something nice that I could cook up for us in the galley for dinner.

As we stood on the deck and bobbed on the water,

the horizon stretching before us, Reuben reached into his pocket and pulled out a small bag. "Would you help me scatter some of Kyle's ashes?" he asked.

I smiled and hugged him close. "Of course."

He pressed a soft kiss to the outside of the bag before opening it up. I placed my hand over his, his gold wedding ring gleaming on his finger as he lifted the bag high and turned it over. The wind caught the small gray pieces and swirled them around and across the water, almost like they were dancing. "Thank you," Reuben said softly, not to me, but to the horizon.

We stood there in silence until the last bits of ash had vanished from sight. Reuben wrapped his arm around my waist. "And thank you for being here with me."

I hugged him close. "Thank *you* for being here for *me*."

A moment later, Reuben turned to me, the most beautiful smile on his lips. "I love you."

My heart warmed, and I stroked his cheek gently with my fingers. "I love you too."

We stood in each other's arms, the future spread out ahead of us. Neither of us knew what that future would be, but that was all right. For right now, we had the present. And that was the perfect place to be.

Author's Note

THANK YOU TO ALL of you who read this book. Alfred, Lord Tennyson wrote in his elegy *In Memorium A.H.H.*, "'Tis better to have loved and lost than never to have loved at all." Grief is the price of love. It is a universal experience, yet the path is different for each person.

I did a lot of research to ensure that I was approaching grief and addiction respectfully and realistically. Some of the resources I found helpful were *Bearing the Unbearable: Love, Loss, and the Heartbreaking Path of Grief* by Joanne Cacciatore, and SAMHSA (Substance Abuse and Mental Health Services Administration, www.samhsa.gov.)

To any of my readers who are dealing with grief or loss, you are not alone. Take care of yourselves, and know that I love you.

About the Author

Kit Barrie (she/her) was raised by pirates in a traveling carnival where she learned how to fly and to weave fantasy into reality. She identifies as chaotic bisexual, with good intentions and questionable methods. She lives in an utterly unfantastical state in the Midwestern United States with some food goblins who might just be cats gobblin' food.

Please visit www.kitbarrie.com or scan the QR code below for more information on Kit and her other available titles.

Additional Titles by Kit Barrie

<u>The Queerly Classic Collection</u>
The Prince on the Lake: A Queer YA Fairy Tale
Midnight Companion: An MM Retelling of The Legend of
Sleepy Hollow
X Marks the Spot: A Gay Retelling of Treasure Island

<u>The Hanenea'a Chronicles</u>
The Goblin Twins
A Study in Scholar
The Gift

<u>Standalones</u>

Where the Sky Meets the Sea: An MM Mer Steampunk Romance

Spinning Out of Control: An MM Monster Romance (Part of the Monster Match series)

Across Space and Time (Part of the Tales From the Tarot series)

Please consider leaving a review on Amazon, Goodreads, or other book review site. Reviews are extremely important for independent authors and are always appreciated.